A KINK IN THE ROAD

A Deadline Cozy Mystery - Book 7

SONIA PARIN

ISBN: 1981167609

ISBN-13: 978-1981167609

Chapter One

"EVE," Jill leaned in and whispered, "I had to pull a lot of strings to get you into the town meeting. Please... I'm begging you, if you have any opinions, try to keep them to yourself. I know you value our friendship."

Eve pressed her hand to her cheek. "Jill, I'm shocked." Actually, she still felt numb.

Eve had been living in Rock-Maine Island for several months but had only recently discovered the town held regular meetings.

At first, she'd blamed herself for the oversight, but then she'd accidentally discovered Jill had been under strict orders from the entire township to keep Eve away from these meetings. Even her aunt Mira had agreed it would be best for Eve to stay away. Annoyingly, she hadn't explained why.

Jill nibbled the edge of her lip. "I'm almost afraid to ask why you're shocked."

"Well, that you would think I'd say something to embarrass

1

you in public and that you'd use our friendship as a bargaining chip." A low blow, Eve thought but suspected Jill had come under a lot of pressure from the town. "You might as well put a muzzle on me."

Jill grinned. "If only I could."

"I really don't understand what you're so worried about. I promise I will behave and I won't hold any of it against you." Eve brushed an imaginary crumb away. The entire town had been in on it. If Eve hadn't accidentally seen the text message on Jill's cell phone reminding her about the meeting, or if she hadn't overheard the conversation Jill had had at the bakery... and at the café, she would still be none the wiser. The moment she'd found out, Eve had badgered Jill, pushing her to get her an invitation thinking that as a business owner in town, she should show an interest.

Eve shook her head, her tone forcefully casual, "I still don't understand why you went to such great lengths to keep me away. My character is above reproach," she said and struggled to keep a straight face. "I'm such a nice person I even brought cupcakes. You must agree it was a thoughtful gesture on my part."

Jill chortled. "You brought cupcakes to show us what we've been missing out on." Shifting in her chair, Jill stared at Eve. "Hey, did you put something in the cupcakes?"

Eve gaped. "What?"

"Did you intentionally or accidentally put something that will give everyone, including me, the runs as payback for conspiring to keep you away from the town meetings?"

So, it had been a conspiracy.

Eve bit back the remark. "I can't win with you. Remind me

again why we're friends?" Eve asked in jest. Despite the ten years' difference in ages, they had clicked right from the start. In all fairness, Jill had stuck with her through the most testing times.

Eve sat back and remembered first meeting the twenty-four year old local artist at her aunt Mira's house, the setting for Eve's first crime scene. In only a few months, they had both been through thick and thin. This was nothing but a bump in the road. Actually, not even a bump. Just a pebble. Eve couldn't make a big deal out of it.

She leaned in to whisper, "Why is Roger McLain referred to as the town elder? He's my age. He can't possibly be older than thirty... something. Maybe thirty-five."

"The wielder of the gavel has always been referred to as the town elder, regardless of age." Jill pressed her finger to her lips. "Hush, he's about to call the meeting to order."

"Isn't that what the gavel is for?" Eve asked.

Jill shrugged. "Roger is rather sensitive to noise. He has a nervous disposition."

"Is this where you spare my feelings by not telling me he thinks my voice is too loud?" Eve whispered.

"It does carry and you do have a tendency to yelp."

"Yelp?" Eve yelped.

Everyone around Eve hushed her.

Roger McLain cleared his throat. Repeatedly and, for some reason, he stared at Eve. "I would like to call this meeting to order and begin by extending a very special welcome to our newest Rock-Maine Island resident."

Eve pressed her hands to her cheeks and broke into a sincere smile of surprise.

So, this was the reason why Jill had kept her away all this time. Everyone had been secretly planning this moment.

A proper welcome to Rock-Maine Island.

If she'd known, she would have baked champagne cupcakes. Although, who needed champagne when she already felt bubbly inside?

Eve grinned. She'd initially come to Rock-Maine Island to visit her aunt Mira. Having arrived at a crossroads in her life, she had also been pondering the idea of spending some time here to sort herself out. She'd been happy to take one day at a time. In the end, deciding to stay and make the island her home had been a no-brainer.

She'd never thought about having an official welcome, but it made sense. This was a small town. Everyone knew everyone, if not by name then by sight. Of course, now that she was on the verge of finally opening her inn, it stood to reason they would all want to give her a special welcome, the occasion inscribed for perpetuity in the town documents.

However, being a new arrival wasn't the only reason for the special mention. She'd had a hand in catching a few killers. In a roundabout way, she had become a keeper of the peace. Some might even see her as a force to be reckoned with.

"So, without further ado, would you all please join me in welcoming William Hunter the Third."

In deference to Roger's sensitivity to noise, everyone clapped softly. Everyone except Eve who didn't want anyone to think she felt even a smidgen of jealousy or disappointment, so she clapped until her hands stung.

Eve couldn't help wondering about this William Hunter the Third person and why he had merited so much attention.

As she searched the audience, Jill jabbed her in the ribs and gestured to Eve's hands. "Please, Eve. Clap softly."

Roger McLain raised his hands and called for attention. "No doubt you will all want to introduce yourselves to William Hunter the Third, but we have some other business to get through..."

Sitting back, Eve continued to search the crowd for the new island favorite. She recognized almost everyone present, mostly by their clothing but also by their poise and physiques. Her eyes bounced along broad shoulders, bony and narrow ones... even twitching shoulders.

When she came across a figure she didn't recognize, she decided it had to be William Hunter the Third.

Her gaze narrowed. She'd never trusted people with hyphenated names or numbers. She'd bet anything he'd added the appendage to further emphasize his lineage and importance.

Eve decided it had to be him, sitting two rows ahead of them. His head almost blocked her view of Mrs. Jorgen, the local historian and retired librarian, and she was a statuesque woman. Also, the way his shirt collar was pulled around his neck, she'd bet anything he was wearing a tie. What sort of person wore a tie to a casual town meeting?

A show-off, that's who!

Someone who considered himself above everyone else.

That was something no one could accuse her of being.

She was regular Eve. Eve of the people.

Some might even say, "Unique Eve. Fabulous Eve," she whispered under her breath. Although, she could be, "Eve Lloyd the First."

Jill jabbed her again. "Hush. People will hear you."

Eve sunk low in her chair and murmured, "Eve the mad innkeeper." Despite denying it, her aunt Mira had written a character based on her, a mad innkeeper who'd turned out to be a spy. She'd been good enough to be portrayed and forever immortalized in fiction. Yet her arrival on the island hadn't earned her the privilege of a special mention or attention.

Eve rolled her eyes. Well, perhaps she had received some attention. Fate had actually played a hand, making sure everyone became acquainted with her.

Within a couple of days of her arrival she'd come under police scrutiny and been suspected of killing her aunt and her ex-husband. How much more attention did she want?

Tucking her feet under her, Eve decided Willie the Third walked a straight and narrow path, always staying on the right side of the law. He'd probably moved to the island because he enjoyed long walks and quiet nights sitting by the fireplace reading the right books. Leather bound, no doubt. She'd bet anything he'd be the type to denigrate Mira's books and label them bodice rippers. In fact, he'd probably already catalogued all the islanders, slotting them into neat little boxes, none worthy of his attention.

Why would someone like him bother attending the town meeting? He had to have known about the special welcome, which meant he thrived on attention, which he would then shun by keeping to himself, while on every other weekend, his wealthy friends would descend from the city. They would murmur among themselves and point at the locals...

Point at her and say, "Oh, yes. There goes the mad innkeeper." The murmured remark earned her another elbow in the ribs from Jill.

Shifting in her chair, Eve put an end to her conjecture about the new island resident and tuned in to Roger's next announcement.

"As discussed in our previous town meeting, Eleanor Parkinson has been engaged to chronicle town life for a month as a lead-up to the spring festival. Needless to say, we must all join forces in representing our little island. This is our moment to shine, people."

A few heads turned Eve's way.

"Did you see that?" Eve murmured.

"What?" Jill asked.

"Clarence Hill just threw me a warning look. What does he think I'll do?" As if to further emphasize whatever point he'd been trying to make, the town optometrist pushed back his glasses and gave her a stiff nod.

"Eleanor Parkinson will be interviewing everyone and observing us as we get on with our daily activities," Roger continued, "Needless to say..."

"If it's needless to say, why is he saying it? And why is he looking at me again?"

"...We want to put our best foot forward. Needless to say, that means no shenanigans."

Eve cupped her hand over her mouth and whispered, "That's

a pointed look if ever I saw one. I can't believe this. He's singling me out."

Jill groaned under her breath. "Eve, please..."

Once again, Roger raised both hands as if about to deliver a sermon. "I can sense everyone is eager to introduce themselves to William, so we'll keep tonight's meeting short. Refreshments have been set up in the back of the hall. Once again, we'd like to thank Beverley Wales for her time and meticulous attention to detail..."

Eve crumbled one of her cupcakes and searched the crowd for a friendly face. She knew she shouldn't feel slighted. Her aunt had lived on the island her entire life and she'd admitted to sometimes feeling like an outsider.

Sighing, Eve nibbled on a crumb. She'd been waiting to introduce herself to the new arrival but every time she approached him, someone beat her to it.

Once again, she edged toward him only to be intercepted by Helena Flanders.

"Hello, Eve." The travel agent smiled warmly.

"Helena. If I didn't know better, I'd think you were trying to keep me away from William."

Helena chuckled. "Would I do that to you?"

"In a heartbeat. Were you in on it too?"

"What on earth are you referring to?" Helena asked.

"Keeping me away from the town meetings."

Helena gave a breezy wave of her hand. "Oh, Eve. Don't take it to heart. No one thought you'd be interested in attending."

"You're being polite, Helena. What you really mean to say is that everyone hoped I wouldn't be interested."

"Well, are you?"

Eve shrugged. "As a matter of fact, yes. After all, I am opening a business here. Contributing to the island's economy has to mean something. Surely."

"Yes, and that's partly what swayed everyone to change their minds. By the way, when are you opening your inn?"

"The workmen are putting the finishing touches to Jill's apartment over the stables. We'll be opening next week with an afternoon tea for everyone."

"I'm surprised you haven't advertised it."

"Notices will go up tomorrow. Jill is still working on them. It will be an open house." Spotting Elsie McAllister, Eve smiled. "One of the local book groups has already secured a spot for their regular meetings."

"Elsie McAllister's Sisters in Crime?"

"You know about them? What am I saying? Of course, you do."

Helena nodded. "She has a soft spot for you. In fact, she was the first to vote for your inclusion in the town meeting, jumping to your defense by saying your involvement in so much murder and mayhem could only add color to island life. Then again, she'd say that."

"Bless her heart. I'll name a cupcake after her."

"Seriously?"

The way she'd been feeling tonight, anyone prepared to stand up for her deserved a good gesture. "Sure. She's earned it."

Helena bit her lip. "I feel dreadful."

Eve scooped in a big breath. "Why?"

"Don't take this the wrong way..." Helena leaned in and whispered, "I was specifically assigned to keep you away from William Hunter."

Eve waited for Helena to laugh. When she didn't, she set her crumbled cupcake down. "You're serious?"

"Sorry. Roger McLain made it a condition to you attending the town meeting. He sees William as a big fish and is afraid someone will scare him away. You see, William purchased the Wiltshire house from Roger's cousin. It's been on the market for years because few people can afford to buy such a large monstrosity. You understand that. If you hadn't purchased Abby's house, it would still be sitting vacant."

"What exactly does this doyen of all that is acceptable and worthy of a special welcome do?" Eve asked.

"Are you saying you haven't heard of him?"

Eve shook her head. "At the risk of being perceived as indifferent and insulated from the wider world, no... I haven't."

"His family is in the international newspaper business. Along with the house, he also purchased the Island Bugle."

The wealthiest resident had always owned the island's newspaper or had had a stake in it. "And here I was harping on about contributing to the island's economy with my little inn." Eve looked around the hall. She'd never seen everyone so animated and switched on. Like bees in a hive.

Deciding it would be best for everyone if she changed the

subject, Eve said, "By the way, thank you for organizing the cruise. I'm surprised you haven't asked about it." It had been several weeks since her return from the cruise she'd taken with her aunt. Eve had since hit the ground running, focusing on getting her inn ready to open for business, and had been so busy she hadn't had time to socialize.

Helena smiled. "The Bugle kept us all up to date. In fact, there was a special daily column devoted to your trip. Didn't you know?"

Eve managed to blink, but no words came to mind. No one had mentioned it. Not even Jill.

Helena gave a small shrug. "There I was having my breakfast and reading the Bugle when your name popped up."

"Which page?"

"Front page. It covered your arrival and first day on the cruise."

"But... how?" Had Jill passed on the information?

"Circulation went up on the second day," Helena continued, "We had people coming in from the mainland to buy it. And those who couldn't get a copy, queued up at the Chin Wag Café to read it there. Cynthia did a roaring trade. Rumor has it, William read about it and paid the island a visit. Within a few hours, he'd purchased the Bugle."

She'd been used as bait to catch the big fish and...

He'd received the warm welcome.

"I feel cheated," she mouthed the words.

"Pardon?" Helena asked.

"Oh, nothing. Here comes Jill." Eve guessed it was her turn to chaperone her.

"So, any opinions about the town chronicler?" Jill asked.

Eve frowned. "Are you actively encouraging me to express my opinions or are you testing me? It's hard to tell."

Jill gave her an impish smile. "I had no idea you were so sensitive."

Eve gave her a lifted eyebrow look that spoke of disdain. "I could say the same about the entire population of Rock-Maine Island."

"Touché. Are we friends again?" Jill asked.

"That depends. Did you know about the Bugle running a daily column reporting my trip?" Eve asked.

Jill shook her head. "I was too busy doing research for you." Jill looked askance. "Fine... Yes. I might have heard something or other."

"And did you also happen to mention anything to anyone about my experience on the cruise?"

Jill gave a small shrug. "I might have let something slip. Everyone wanted to know how you were faring on your trip. They care about you, Eve."

"Admit it, they're only interested in the entertainment I can provide. Well, no more." Eve raised her chin and smiled brightly. "I'll be far too busy running my inn. Which reminds me. We have our first staff meeting in a couple of days. Also... I should get going." She raised her voice slightly and looked around her, a part of her wanting to let everyone know she hadn't been affected by their behavior toward her because she was far too busy to care. "I promised Mira I'd be back in time to... to discuss a dinner party she's planning... for her editor. Her New York editor."

"You're back early, Eve."

Eve strode into the living room and smiled at Mira. "I would have returned earlier, but that would have been rude. Especially after all the trouble everyone went to, holding a town meeting to decide if I should be allowed to attend a town meeting."

Mira chuckled under her breath.

She joined her aunt on the couch. The book-lined room, with its comfortable chairs and plump cushions, had become her favorite room in the house. The sun had set and the table lamps cast a soft light. The windows offered an uninterrupted view of the beach, not that she could see much of it now, but she had enjoyed many nights gazing out to sea and the twinkling stars.

Eve stretched her legs out and yawned. "By the way, you're having a dinner party."

"I am? Did I forget to make a note of it?" Mira asked.

"You might have. You know how you get when you're in your writing cave." Eve inspected her fingernails. "Also, you're inviting your editor."

Mira's eyes widened slightly. "Why would I do that?"

"Because... because I need to do a practice run at the inn and that requires some special people. The type I might want to impress. She can stay at the inn."

"She? I could have sworn my editor was a man." Mira set the book she'd been reading down and picked up her diary. "Yes. Here it is. Monday, call Jordan."

"Fine, it's a man. I always thought Jordan was a woman. You

never specified. In fact, it's always been Jordan this and Jordan that."

"Remind me again why he's coming to dinner?"

Eve kicked off her loafers. "Oh, never mind all that. If you must know, I'm a bit..." she clicked her fingers, "What's that word your mad innkeeper always uses? Cross. Yes, that's it. I'm a bit cross with everyone for thinking I'm incapable of behaving in public."

"And did you, dare I ask, behave in public?" Mira asked.

Eve leaned back on the couch and rolled her head from side to side. "Sort of."

"And what did you think about our new arrival?"

Eve sprung upright. "You know about him?"

Mira nodded. "I bumped into him at the Chin Wag Café. Roger McLain introduced us, and we sat down for a coffee."

"I see the embargo doesn't include you." Eve folded her arms across her chest. "I wasn't allowed to talk to him."

"Why would I be banned from talking to him? I'm perfectly normal."

Eve grabbed a cushion and pressed it against her face to stifle her groan.

"Don't take it so hard, Eve. You haven't missed anything. He's just a run of the mill billionaire. Too much money and time on his hands. The Bugle is nothing but a hobby for him. I remember thinking he'd be a perfect candidate for murder."

"Mira!"

"I'm only making conversation. It's fine when it's just the two of us." Mira picked up her mug and inspected it.

"What are you drinking? I'll make you another cup," Eve offered.

"Tea, thank you. Chamomile. I need a good night's rest."

"Is your new book giving you trouble?"

"Oh, no dear. Thinking about William Hunter and how long he'll last will keep me tossing and turning all night, I'm sure of it."

"He should be fine. Everyone is circling the wagons around him," Eve said as she strode out of the living room.

"Something tells me that won't be enough."

"I heard that."

Chapter Two

EVE SET a platter of freshly baked muffins on the table and bent down to give Mr. Magoo and Mischief a hello scratch behind the ears. As Jill's Labradors would always be welcomed at the inn, she had decided to make it pet friendly.

With that thought in mind, she grabbed her notepad and scribbled a reminder to be more specific.

Yes to dogs. No to exotic pets.

She didn't see any harm in being specific. Just in case someone got the wrong idea and decided to bring their pet Python on vacation.

Straightening, she sent her gaze skating around the large kitchen table. "Thank you all for coming this morning."

Jill looked around her. "It's just you and me, Eve."

Eve smiled. "I wanted to start the way I mean to go on. Samantha will be along shortly. She called earlier to say she needed to open *Tinkerbelle's* first." Thank goodness for

Samantha Beckett, Eve thought. She'd been trying to fill the spot of assistant manager for a couple of weeks with no success.

While Samantha loved working at the bookstore Mira had purchased in town, she'd expressed an interest in spreading her wings and getting some experience in the hospitality industry. Since Samantha shared her job with Aubrey Leeds who could step in and work extra hours, Mira had been only too happy to agree to give Samantha time off, but only until Eve could find someone else to manage the front desk. "The kitchen and serving staff will join our meetings in a couple of days. I need to get back into the swing of things. Bear with me, please. This is a practice run and I want to avoid the bad habit of only looking at one person."

Jill looked around. "Your absent employees are all in agreement."

"Go ahead, make fun of me." Eve put a tick on the first order of business and turned the page. "Announcements. Are the posters for the afternoon tea ready?"

Jill signaled to a box she'd set on the table. "I've organized a couple of local kids to do a mailbox drop and I'll be posting the posters around town myself. I'm hoping to bump into the town chronicler so we can have our first official mention."

"Fantastic. Thank you for doing that. Next on the agenda. I've talked Mira into having a dinner party. I'm thinking Friday night, so I'll be working on a menu today." Which took care of keeping her away from town and any chance of bumping into his lordship. "We'll also have our first official guest. Jordan Monroe, Mira's editor. I'll book him in for the weekend. That should give us a good three days to get into the rhythm of things."

"How many people are attending the dinner party?"

"I'm not sure yet. There's Mira. I suppose I could ask Helena. She has a discerning palate. I have some game dishes in mind I'd like her to try. Abby Larkin is visiting the island. She's keen to see what we've done with her house."

"Will she be staying here?" Jill asked.

"She's still thinking about it. The last time I spoke with her she was having second thoughts about staying in an inn where someone had been murdered."

Jill gave her a brisk smile. "Two people, at last count. Not that I'm keeping track." Jill took a nibble of her muffin. "Yum. Blueberry and lemon. These will be a hit."

"Thank you. Next on my list, advertising. I've placed listings in several weekend getaways magazines. They'll appear early next week. Fingers crossed, we should start getting some phone calls by the end of the week. Samantha will have to be on her toes. We want to screen our guests."

Jill nodded. "No ghost hunters or anyone expressing an interest in the murders."

"I thought we'd decided to call them incidents."

"Sorry. Incidents."

"Next item on the agenda. Clothing. After some careful consideration, I'm inclined to agree with you. We should keep it casual. Meaning, no uniforms." Eve drummed her fingers on the table. "Is Josh available this weekend? I wouldn't mind having him around the place." Jill's police officer boyfriend had briefly acted as grounds keeper during an early practice run when a film crew had taken over the house. They would only have one guest and while Eve wouldn't expect Josh to actually work, she would feel more comfortable with him around. If anything were to happen to Mira's editor, she'd never hear the end of it. Eve worried her bottom lip as she watched Jill place a call.

"Yes." Jill disconnected the call and nodded. "Josh has a few free days coming up and he's more than happy to spend them working."

"Are you trying to keep a straight face?" Eve asked.

Jill nodded. "I'm doing my best. Josh had been looking forward to kicking back and relaxing but I told him he didn't have a choice."

"Okay. I'll go easy on him. I'm sure he'll have plenty of time to relax. We'll only have the one guest."

Jill's cell phone rang. "It's Josh. He probably came up with a sound argument and will try to talk me out of forcing him to do this. I'll take it outside. Mischief and Mr. Magoo could do with a run along the beach." Before she stepped out the back door, Jill turned. "Eve."

"Yes?"

"About the other night at the town meeting..."

The front door bell chimed. "Think nothing of it. I'm too busy to give William Hunter the Third a second thought."

"Yes, but... I can't help feeling we were all unfair to you. I wish I hadn't gone along with everyone. In fact, I'm going to make it my business to tell anyone who mentions it off. As far as I'm concerned, I'm the only one allowed to censor you."

Mr. Magoo whimpered.

Jill cringed. "Okay. I just heard myself. Sorry."

"You needn't worry about me. I'm staying well away from Willie III. I'm too busy to think about a stiff necked oligarch."

Jill tilted her head. "Is that what he is?"

"I'm sure of it. Newspaper moguls are usually influential in the upper echelons of society. I say ho-hum to that."

As Eve went to answer the door, she gave herself a mental pat on the back. Their first official meeting had gone smoothly. It reminded Eve of the days she'd worked as a chef in her own Manhattan restaurant where everything had run on schedule and in perfect harmony. This was her milieu, her ideal comfort zone. Eve nodded. Yes, everything would work out as planned.

"Eve Lloyd?" the woman at the door asked.

"Yes, that's me."

"I'm Elizabeth Rogue. William Hunter's personal assistant."

Eve glanced over her shoulder to make sure Jill hadn't come back inside. Playing it safe, she stepped outside. As she did, she couldn't help noticing the surprise on Elizabeth Rogue's perfectly made up face.

A tall woman in her late twenties, she wore a pair of charcoal black tailored trousers matched with a cream blouse. Noticing the fine sheen on the fabric, Eve decided the blouse had to be made of real silk. A single strand of pearls hung around her neck. Eve guessed they were not cultured, but rather, the real deal.

Although young, Elizabeth Rogue presented herself with flair and an air of sophistication one normally acquired with age.

"Lovely to meet you. How can I help you?" Eve asked.

"I wanted to confirm a booking."

Confirm? "We're not actually open for business yet."

"I tried to call but you don't seem to be listed," Elizabeth Rogue said, "In fact, I asked around town and no one could tell me the name of your inn."

Jill's latest suggestion, Hangman's Noose, nearly tripped out but Eve managed to contain it. "It's The Sea Breeze Inn." At least that had been the last safe choice they'd come up with. An improvement on Work-in-Progress Inn.

"Lovely." Elizabeth Rogue checked her planner. "We've been told Friday lunch would be fine. We have a party of five, although that could change at any minute."

"That can't be right. We're not taking bookings yet."

Elizabeth Rogue checked her planner again and smiled. "Mira Lloyd assured us we could be accommodated."

Mira?

"In fact, she said the more the merrier."

She had?

"So if you give me your contact details, I'll call later in the day with exact numbers. I trust you'll have an acceptable selection of wines..." Elizabeth Rogue checked her watch. "We look forward to the experience." Without waiting for Eve to respond, she turned and made her way to her sporty car.

"In all fairness, the person responsible for committing the crime should do the time," Eve mused even though she knew she couldn't ask Mira to call Elizabeth Rogue and explain there had been a mistake. What on earth had possessed her aunt? If Eve didn't know better, she'd suspect Mira had been trying to stir things up a bit.

"What are you muttering about?" Jill asked as she strode

back in, Mr. Magoo and Mischief at her heels, their tails wagging and their tongues lolling.

"Me? Oh... I was wondering if I should... have my hair cut for the photo shoot."

"It'll just be me behind the camera, Eve. Hardly a photo shoot."

"You're a professional artist. Never sell yourself short, Jill. Anyhow, I'm thinking I should stand in front of my stunningly gorgeous Grand Palais 180." She gave her brand new stove a loving caress. The bespoke stove had been as expensive as a luxury car, but worth every penny.

"I'm still surprised it managed to fit inside the kitchen. It's... imposing. I might have to get a special camera lens to fit it into the frame." Jill washed her hands and grabbed another muffin. "But I'm sure I heard you muttering about something else."

Eve wiped an imaginary smudge from the counter. Her shoulders lifted and dropped. With a sigh of resignation, she turned to face Jill. "You've known me long enough to learn all about best laid plans."

"Should I sit down for this?" Jill held her gaze for several seconds. "Yes, I feel I should sit down."

Eve gave a stiff nod. "Yes, you might want to." Raking her fingers through her hair, she sighed again. "You know what this inn means to me and how much I want it to succeed. Nothing can go wrong."

"And nothing will. We've already agreed to adopt a positive attitude." Jill nibbled on her muffin. "We've also acknowledged the fact we can't control all outcomes." Jill waved her hand around. "But our stalwart determination will help us navigate through the roughest waters."

"Quit mocking me and be serious for a moment."

Jill sat up. "Okay. You have my full attention."

Eve squared her shoulders and lifted her chin. "There has been an unexpected development and it will pose a challenge."

Jill slid to the edge of the chair and gaped at her. "But I was only gone five minutes. What could possibly have happened in that time?"

"Yes, well... Our best laid plans have been tampered with."

"It can't be a body," Jill's voice quivered, "Please tell me it's not a body. Was it the mailman? I know he sometimes gets the addresses wrong, but that's no reason for someone to kill him..."

"Please, calm down, Jill. You're making me jittery." Eve brushed her hands across her face. She should have said no. Well, she had said no. In reality, she should have been firm. In her shoes, someone like Elizabeth Rogue, with her tailored pants, silk blouse and string of pearls, would have stood her ground, suffering no fools.

As a chef, Eve had been trained to be firm. Decisive. Even bossy. But how would it look if she turned down the island's favorite son?

"Is something wrong with Jill?" Mira asked. "She looks like one of those cute little Meerkats, standing sentry, ready to warn of approaching danger. I've been here half an hour and in all that time she hasn't stood still. She must be wearing out the veranda and her head turns this way and that way. She'll get whiplash."

Eve brought the cleaver down making a clean cut through a joint. She turned the chicken over and began work on the other half. "Don't worry about her," Eve said matter-of-factly. "She's been drinking too much coffee."

"I swear she jumped out of her skin just now when you brought the cleaver down."

Eve wiped her hands dry.

"And is that a walkie-talkie she's carrying?"

Eve nodded. "She forgot to charge her cell phone so Josh brought those along to use."

"You'd think a head of state was visiting," Mira mused.

Eve sighed. "We've decided to take certain precautions."

Mira set her cup of tea down. "Jordan will be impressed. He's accustomed to staying in nice hotels so I told him not to expect much."

"Trust me. He'll be given the full royal treatment, and then some..."

The sound of a whistle blowing had them both looking out the window in time to see Jill jumping off the back veranda and running up the beach, her arms flapping by her sides.

"Heavens. What now?" Mira asked.

Leaning over to see what might have caught Jill's attention, Eve saw a couple of locals striding along the beach with their two dogs trailing behind.

Mira gasped. "What can that possibly be about?"

"Jill's created a no-go zone around the inn," Eve said calmly, "Like I said, we're taking precautions."

"What sort of precautions? Are you going to cordon off the inn?"

Eve looked up and thought for a moment. "That might not be such a bad idea."

"And hire security?"

Again, Eve looked pensive. "That could work too. Josh is here for the weekend, but that might not be enough manpower."

"You're serious. What's brought all this on?"

Eve bit her lip. No point in crying over spilled milk... What was done could not be undone. She looked heavenward. Any minute now and she'd break into a chorus of platitudes.

"If you must know..." No, she shouldn't say anything. She couldn't.

"Yes?"

Eve shook her head. "Oh, don't worry about it, Mira."

"I suppose if I bide my time and sit here long enough, you'll spill everything. I know you, Eve. You can't contain yourself for long."

"Hey, I can keep secrets."

Mira wagged her finger at her. "But you're not keeping a secret. Oh, no. I can sense it. This is something entirely different. Something that has you and Jill all worked up." Mira frowned and half rose up from her chair. "Is that the sound of police sirens?"

The sirens drew closer. Within minutes, they heard the pounding of footsteps on the front veranda and, in the next moment, Jack burst in through the front door and called out, "Eve."

"In the kitchen," Eve said, her tone light and cheerful.

Detective Jack Bradford rushed into the kitchen. "What's happened? Is everyone all right?"

Before Eve could answer, Jill came in through the back door, Mr. Magoo and Mischief rushing in ahead of her, their eyes bright with excitement.

"What took you so long?" Jill demanded, "I called you two minutes ago. If we can't rely on the local law enforcement, what hope do we have?"

"Would you mind explaining what's going on?" Jack asked. Strangely, he turned to Eve as if she alone could provide a sound explanation.

Eve gave him a brisk smile. "Isn't it obvious. Jill wanted to test your response to an emergency."

Jack held her gaze for several seconds and then raked his fingers through his hair. Eve had met him shortly after her arrival on the island and they'd now been together for a few months. By now, she had acquired the ability to read the signs. Jack was calling on all his reserves to remain calm.

"What emergency?" he asked.

Eve pressed her lips together. If she answered, then Mira would put two and two together and realize she'd been responsible for triggering this all hands on deck commotion.

Jill's arms flailed about. "What emergency? The one we're going to have because there is no getting away from it now. It's inevitable." Jill paced around the kitchen. "But if we play our cards right, we might... maybe... hopefully, we might just manage to contain the situation."

Jack's gaze danced between Eve and Jill. Finally, it settled on

Eve. "You seem to be uncharacteristically calm. Would you mind explaining what's going on?"

"Fine." Eve washed her hands and took her time drying them. "Someone is going to be murdered."

"Who?" Mira and Jack asked, their tones full of intrigue and unwavering interest.

Eve shrugged and casually said, "We're not sure yet."

Jack switched over to detective mode. His face relaxed and his tone became matter-of-fact crisp. "Have you received a threat?"

Eve tilted her head. "No."

"Did you overhear a conversation?"

"No."

"Have you seen someone suspicious hanging around?"

"Not yet," Jill piped in. "But I have that covered. Josh is upstairs with his binoculars. If anyone comes within a mile of the inn, I'll know." As if to confirm how well she had everything covered, Jill waved her walkie-talkie.

"Would anyone like some coffee?" Eve offered. "Not you, Jill. I think you've had enough."

Mira smiled. "I wouldn't mind an Irish Coffee. I think I could do with a shot of whiskey right about now. Jack, I know you're on duty so you might want to try a cup of chamomile tea."

"Thanks for the suggestion, Mira. But first, I'd like a word with Eve. In the den, please."

Wiping her hands dry again even though they weren't wet, she followed him. Jack went to stand by the fireplace, his gaze fixed on a spot on the floor.

"Is Jill all right?" he asked.

Eve gave a breezy wave of her hand. "Oh, sure. She's fine."

"She doesn't sound it."

"It's nothing but a case of... overreacting."

"To what?"

"I suppose forewarned is forearmed." Sighing, Eve sunk down on the couch and, looking around the room, she gave a nod of approval. The workmen had done a fine job polishing the floorboards, and the plantation shutters had been a great choice as she could adjust them throughout the day to keep any direct sunlight away from the bookcases. "We believe something will happen... shortly. Perhaps within the next twenty-four to forty-eight hours."

"And you know this because..."

Eve shrugged. "It's just a hunch."

"Is this about Jill accusing you of being a death knell? That was so long ago, Eve. I thought you were over it."

"Oh, no. We're both over that. Jill and I have simply come to accept the inevitable."

Jack sighed. "Walk me through your reasoning."

Eve looked over her shoulder to make sure she'd remembered to close the door. It wouldn't do for Mira to overhear the conversation.

"There's a newcomer on the island. Everyone's tried to keep me away from him." Sensing Jack wanted to ask why, she shrugged. "It seems I have acquired a reputation as a trouble-maker. Before you say anything, I made a point of staying away from town, but now..." She told him about the visit she'd had from Elizabeth Rogue and the arrangements she'd been forced to make because Mira had taken it upon herself to spread the word about the inn. "I don't want Mira to make the connection and feel responsible for Jill's overreaction."

Jack shook his head. "Mira's a big girl. She can take it. But if the thought of holding a lunch for the newcomer is going to cause so much trouble and worry, why not cancel it?"

Eve lifted her chin. "This has become a matter of pride. If I turn him away, I'll be cultivating an attitude of suspicion. Instead of focusing on the occupancy rate, I'll be obsessing about the survival rate at my inn." She tapped her chin. "Do you think I should instal surveillance cameras? At least in the hallways."

"It would be advisable. However, I doubt your guests would appreciate being recorded."

She tilted her head back and stared up at the ceiling. "Can dogs be trained to detect killers? I'm sure they give off a scent."

Jack chuckled. "Not that I know of." He brushed his hands across his face. "So, all this is about you and Jill taking pre-emptive action."

"It's actually more Jill's doing. She has my back and she means well." Eve rose to her feet. "I'm sorry we dragged you into this. Would you like a coffee now? You can come and admire my new stove."

"Eve, if I didn't know better, I'd think you were either hitting the bottle or popping happy pills."

"Oh," Eve waved her hand, the gesture dismissive, "I'm on the verge of doing both."

Chapter Three

IT'S ONLY LUNCH, Eve told herself. Two or three hours at most and then, her unwanted guests would be out of her hair and she could jump right back into the steady flow she had created for herself.

Smiling, she drew in a steadying breath and sang under her breath, "I will row, row, row my boat, gently down the stream because life really is nothing but a—"

Jill entered the kitchen, her pace brisk, and her tone businesslike. "The guests are all seated and chatting amiably. That would be an encouraging sign, but we both know killers are cunning. We can, however, relax a little. I've studied them closely and did not detect any signs of pre-existing conditions, which might have posed a problem since we don't want anyone keeling over from natural causes either."

"You did a visual health check," Eve said flatly.

Jill gave a stiff nod. "When I make my statement to the

police, I want to include as much information as possible. And, for the record, I feel you were wrong not to ask Jack to come. He would have been an excellent addition at the table. I had it all figured out in my mind. I can still picture him putting his police issue revolver on the table and daring anyone to make a false move."

"Detective Jack Bradford for hire as a lunch guest peacekeeper. There's a thought." Eve managed a chuckle. "At ease soldier."

Appearing to relax, Jill smiled. "Are you sure you don't wish them to sign a waiver expunging you from any and all liability and or culpability? I've already drafted something out for you."

Giving Jill a roll of her eyes, Eve tasted the salad dressing for tanginess. She'd caught a glimpse of William Hunter as Samantha Becket had greeted him and his party of seven, which included his assistant, Elizabeth Rogue.

Thank goodness Samantha had agreed to step in and act as hostess for the day. Mira had happily given her the day off from the bookstore. Eve couldn't help thinking she'd caught a glint of chomping at the bit excitement in her aunt's eyes. Shaking her head, Eve thought Mira would argue in favor of champing at the bit, instead of chomping. She entertained the distracting thought for a moment and then resumed thinking about the island's new favorite son.

When she'd caught a glimpse of him, William had looked perfectly at ease, his golden hair slightly mussed by the sea breeze that had been whipping around all morning.

He'd been dressed in *über*-rich casual attire, with a white shirt, a blue blazer with an emblem embroidered on the pocket, but no tie this time. She'd expected him to have a booming voice but had been disappointed by the drone like tone she'd heard.

All would be well, Eve assured herself as she gazed out the kitchen window. She had everything under control. With Jill's help, she would deal with this. Even the weather was in her favor.

She could already see clouds gathering in the horizon—a prelude to the storm that had been forecasted. Thunder and lightning. Just what they needed to add to the ambiance. Everyone would surely want to hurry back home as soon as they could.

"Okay. Let's get cracking." Eve set a pitcher of water on a tray. "Jill, I followed your suggestion and personally washed the pitcher several times to cleanse it of any residual poisonous substances that might have found their way in, deliberately or by accident, and I filled it with bottled water." A case of it had been delivered earlier that day; the note attached explaining William only drank that particular brand. Eve had heard about the exclusive and astronomically priced water but she'd had to do a quick search online to learn it was priced at over $400 a bottle. More expensive than the finest French Champagne. Some people clearly had more money than good sense. This begged the question...

Why bother having lunch at an inn when he could clearly afford to have a chef flown in from Paris?

Jill put her hand up. "Would you like me to taste the water? I think that would look good in the witness statement."

"Jill, there is not going to be a witness statement because no one is going to be murdered." Besides, she'd inspected the bottles herself subjecting them to a thorough scrutiny. The seals had been intact.

Shaking her head, Jill said, "You say that with so much confidence."

Eve frowned. "And you almost sound disappointed."

"You're right." Jill lifted her chin. "No more expecting the worst to happen. The guests will enjoy a splendid lunch and then be on their way. You don't have to have any contact with them. In fact, you don't even have to step out of the kitchen."

Eve didn't intend to. She would remain within the safety of her kitchen domain for the duration of the meal. She had even taken precautions, making Mira promise to do all she could to stop Eve from wandering off.

Hearing the back door open, they turned in time to see Mira returning from her walk along the beach, her cheeks flushed slightly.

"Oh, I missed the guests' arrival," Mira said, "Are they all still alive?"

Scooping in a fortifying breath, Eve called for calm. "May I have everyone's attention, please?" she said as Samantha joined them.

The twenty-five year old had gathered her honey blonde hair into an elegant chignon. While Eve hadn't expected her to dress up for her impromptu role as hostess, she had been instantly impressed by Samantha's neat and tidy appearance. The young girl had chosen to wear a slate gray pair of slacks matched with a patterned blouse in pale shades of green. "We are entertaining lunch guests and offering them a simple yet satisfying experience. We are not prepping them for murder. Is that understood?"

Jill shrugged, "You said it yourself, Eve. Your best laid plans have been tampered with."

Mira looked sheepish. "Yes, about that... I am sorry, Eve. I don't know what came over me."

"No, neither do I," Eve agreed, "I thought you were on a deadline. Isn't it enough you have a mad innkeeper to amuse you?"

"I'm afraid I've written myself into a corner." Mira shrugged. "I need some fresh inspiration. Anyhow, when the temptation presented itself, I simply couldn't help wandering what would happen if William Hunter orbited closer to you."

Eve raised her hands and called for all that was good in the universe to guard and guide her.

Jill leaned in and whispered to Mira, "Is she blessing or cursing us?"

"It's hard to say." Mira smiled. "Eve, I'd offer to leave but I promised you I'd watch over you. Just in case you need an alibi."

Samantha stepped forward. "I've served the snacks. Smoked almonds, marinated olives and the platter of charcuteries with crusty bread." She held up a piece of paper. "These are their aperitif orders."

That had been the only concession Eve had allowed the lunch guests. When Elizabeth Rogue had called with final numbers, Eve had set her foot down, agreeing she would go through with the lunch on the condition they accept a chef's choice tasting menu, with no alterations or additions. As she had a reasonably well-stocked bar, she had allowed them the freedom to order whatever drinks they wanted.

Jill rolled up her sleeves. "I got this." She glanced at Eve and received a nod of approval.

Jill's role at the inn hadn't been defined yet. Eve felt reluctant to distract her from her artistic endeavors, but Jill seemed intent on learning as much as she could, just in case she ever needed a fall-back job.

"While you fix the drinks, I'm going to work on the starters." Eve had spent the morning preparing the saffron scented leek and potato soup while the day before had been devoted to making the pork and pistachio terrine and chicken liver parfait.

The inn had been on lockdown with only Eve, Jill and Josh present, and now Mira. All the food being served had been prepared by Eve, including the bread, which she had baked earlier that morning. Her new stove had been getting a thorough workout.

She had enough to keep her busy in the kitchen giving her no reason to venture out into the dining area, Eve thought as she checked her schedule. Everything had been timed with precision. Nothing had been left to chance, she thought as she set the soup bowls in a neat row and inspected them for smudges.

"So far so good," Jill announced moments later as she returned from serving the drinks. "I've checked with Josh and all is well. Let's hope they don't linger over their coffees. That storm is not moving away. We wouldn't want them to be stranded here."

"You're getting a bit ahead of yourself," Mira remarked, "They've yet to have their starters."

"Eve's worked it all out." Jill pointed at the schedule written on the kitchen whiteboard. "Ten more minutes and I'll start serving the entrées."

"Tell me about William's guests," Mira encouraged. "I'd go out there to see for myself, but I don't dare leave Eve alone."

"Well... There's William's ex-wife, the super model Valentine. They're going to give it another go so she is also his current fiancée. Liz Logan, also his ex-wife. Miranda Leeds, another ex. Stew Peters. He sounds like the proverbial detractor in the group. So far, I've heard nothing but complaints from him. He doesn't like the sea. The drive here took too long. A seagull squawked at him." Jill shrugged. "Then there's Marcus Leeds, Miranda's current husband. And... Julia Maeve. She's a senior editor at one of William's newspapers. Oh, and Elizabeth Rogue. William's personal assistant."

Mira glanced at Eve. "You have to admire a man who remains friends with his ex-wives and is even prepared to remarry one of them."

Eve refrained from commenting; silently insisting the kitchen had to remain neutral ground.

With the starters on their way, she checked the time and took a few moments to tidy up before preparing the main course.

Mira sighed. "Well. That's quite a collection of people. Three ex-wives. Some of those names ring bells. I've heard say Valentine has an unpredictable temper. At some point, I will have to take a peek. From what I hear, Liz Logan and Julia Maeve don't get along, at all."

Eve strode over to the adjoining sunroom and sunk down on the couch next to Mischief and Mr. Magoo. She'd had a devil of a time explaining to the health inspectors the dogs were well trained and would never stray away from their designated area.

"I hope your editor arrives before it starts to rain," Eve said, "I wouldn't want him to get caught driving in bad weather." Leaning back, she closed her eyes and smiled, taking a moment to enjoy the silence.

All the details had been worked out. Nothing would go wrong. In a few hours, they would be on their merry way.

Jill's walkie-talkie crackled. "Code blue. Code blue."

Groaning softly, Eve peeled an eye open.

"What on earth is that?" Mira asked, "And what is code blue?"

"Jill wanted ready access to Josh. She says the walkie-talkie is more efficient than using a cell phone." Hauling herself back to the kitchen, Eve picked up the walkie-talkie and casually answered, "What's up, Josh?"

"A car pulled up outside the inn. A woman is getting out. Going by the way she wrenched her sunglasses off, I'd say she's not happy. Wait... she's making a beeline for the front door. Someone needs to intercept her. There's a bulge in her pocket. It appears to be weighing the coat down. I suspect it's a revolver."

Keeping her tone casual, Eve said, "Thank you for the update. Samantha will take care of it."

"She might need backup," Josh suggested, "I'm on my way downstairs. Don't tell Jill I've abandoned my post."

"I suggest you stay put, Josh."

He sighed. "Yeah, you're probably right. Over and out."

"Is that really Josh?" Mira asked.

"Yes. That's... Officer Josh Matthews moonlighting as..." Eve shrugged. "Never mind."

Moments later, Jill strode into the kitchen and chirped, "We have a late arrival. Martha Payne. Elizabeth Rogue apologizes for the inconvenience. Martha hadn't responded to the invitation. Apparently, she enjoys just turning up and making a fuss. I assured Elizabeth Rogue we could accommodate another lunch guest."

Eve plastered on a smile. "Sure. As Mira said, the more the merrier."

Jill cleared her throat. "I should warn you. She is carrying a weapon."

Eve blinked. She searched her mind for an appropriate response. When she drew a blank, she wondered if that was the first sign of a fatal disease...

"When I took her coat," Jill explained, "I took the liberty of patting the pockets. Finding the revolver, I asked her about it. She has a permit."

"Well, that's a relief," Mira mused. "Is she, by any chance, another ex-wife?"

"Yes, how did you know?"

"A lucky guess."

Jill peered out the window. "Those thunder clouds are getting closer."

Jill scurried into the kitchen, grabbed a dish towel, and scuttled out again without saying a word.

Eve and Mira exchanged a raised eyebrow look but didn't say anything.

The hum of conversation coming from the dining room sounded cheerful enough. Eve guessed someone must have spilled something.

Mira eventually broke the silence. "Something smells wonderful, Eve. My mouth is watering."

Eve smiled. "This stove is fantastic. It does everything, including barbecuing." She cut the potatoes into neat slices and precise strips, making sure they were all the same length. After rinsing them in cold water, she placed them in a pan and brought them to the boil. She spent the next five minutes wiping down surfaces and making sure everything would be ready for the main course.

Draining the potatoes, she dried them thoroughly before blanching them in a deep fryer. Setting them aside to drain on paper towels, she began preparing the plates.

Jill rushed in again. "Do we have any pink salt?"

Eve handed her a small grinder.

Jill looked at it. "When Valentine asked for pink salt, I thought she was making it up but I didn't dare contradict her. She's... She's scary." Jill waved and scampered out again.

"I thought you seasoned your food to perfection," Mira remarked.

"I do."

"That TV chef who swears a lot wouldn't stand for someone adding salt to his food."

"Mira, are you baiting me?"

"No, dear. Why would I do that?"

Eve dropped the fries into the deep fryer and cooked them until they were golden and crisp.

She estimated it would take the guests half an hour to forty-five minutes to eat the main, depending on how much talking and drinking they did. The hum of conversation wafted from the dining room. So far, it all sounded perfectly civilized and, despite the odd group of people at the table, Eve had no reason to believe anything would disrupt the peace.

Jill appeared just as Eve finished inspecting each plate. "All good to go."

Without saying a word, Jill picked up the mains and hurried out into the dining room.

"Weren't you going to get some serving staff?" Mira asked.

"Jill insisted she could handle it. In her opinion, the less people who come into contact with the food, the better." Eve shrugged. "Less suspects for the police to worry about." She really needed to stop stoking the fire. In days to come, she would look back on all this and have a good laugh at her own expense. But right that minute... She was hanging by a thread and struggling to avoid thinking of everything that could still go wrong.

Mira checked her watch. "Jordan should be arriving soon. You needn't worry about him. I'll entertain him. And you'll want to take a break before tonight's dinner."

"Yes, I plan on having a nice soak in the bathtub," Eve said as she arranged the final plates for Jill to collect. As Jill made quick work of carrying them out, Eve edged toward the door leading to the dining room and peered out.

The nods of approval she saw were enough to satisfy her.

Finally, she could breathe easy.

Clearing the kitchen bench, Eve strode around the counter, poured two glasses of wine and handed one to Mira.

Mira raised her glass in a salute. "Well done, Eve."

Eve took a sip of her wine, enjoying the full-bodied flavor with hints of blackcurrant.

"All those ex-wives sitting at the same table," Mira commented, "I wonder what keeps them coming back for more? I've met the man. Sure, he's good-looking, but he's as dull as dishwater."

Eve took another sip.

"Maybe they've all come together to plot his murder," Mira added.

Eve tipped the glass back and drank deeply.

"That would be an interesting twist. Here you are, trying to avoid the man and he lands right on your doorstep bringing an entourage of possible murderers with him."

The walkie-talkie crackled. "Amber alert. Repeat. Amber alert. Two people are headed toward the house. Now they've reached the gate and they're splitting up. One is striding along the west side of the house, the other one appears to be making a beeline for the kitchen..."

Ignoring Mira's wide-eyed expression, Eve poured herself another glass of wine. As she took a sip, she looked out the window and nearly choked.

"Is that Elsie McAllister from the Sisters in Crime reading group?" Mira waved at Elsie, but the woman ducked, presumably to avoid detection.

"Yes," Eve said flatly.

"What is she doing out there?" Mira looked at Eve. "You're frowning. What's wrong?"

Did she really need to ask? "I'm searching for a word." She took another sip of her wine.

"The nips are getting bigger?"

"Pardon?"

"It's an Australian expression." She eyed Eve's glass. "It means you're having more and more to drink. Not that I'm judging. In fact, you have dealt with all this admirably well."

"I'm not celebrating until they've had their coffees and gone on their way." Eve took another sip. "Perverse. That's the word I was hunting for."

"In what context were you thinking about it?"

"Delight. As in, despite everyone's reservations, I'd bet anything the locals are showing a perverse delight in all this and are waiting for something to happen." She raised her glass. "But nothing will happen. We've made sure of that."

"Code red. Code red."

Eve nearly dropped her glass.

"That sounds rather urgent," Mira said as she offered to top Eve's glass.

"Just a finger, please."

The walkie-talkie crackled. "Is anyone there?"

Eve's eye twitched. "Actually, make that two fingers."

"Shouldn't we do something about that?" Mira asked, her voice full of innocence.

Eve held the glass against her mouth and pretended to give the idea some thought before shaking her head. "I'm sure it's nothing."

"I repeat, code red," Josh's voice sounded breathless. "Everyone to their battle stations. I repeat. Code red."

Eve rolled her eyes and held her glass out. "Go ahead. Top it up to the rim."

Jill burst into the kitchen. "What's happened? I thought I heard Josh."

Right on cue, they heard the sound of a whistle being blown.

Jill plunged her fingers through her hair. "That's the last resort alarm. Why didn't you call me?"

Eve nudged a stool with her foot. "You look run off your feet, Jill. Take a load off."

"Take a break? How can you suggest that when there's a code red happening?" Jill flapped her arms and rushed off, presumably to meet up with Josh and deal with the code red.

"Should we follow?" Mira half rose out of her chair.

Eve wagged her finger. "I have no intention of leaving this kitchen unattended and your job is to supervise me." As far as Eve was concerned, she had a duty of care but that only involved making sure no one died from her food. Anything else remained strictly out of her control.

Mira sank back down on her chair.

Seeing Mira's disappointment, Eve said, "I'm sure Jill will return with news."

The walkie-talkie crackled again. They heard Jill yelp and Josh grunt. The sounds of a scuffle were followed by silence.

Mira strode over to the window. "I think they've wrestled someone to the ground."

Eve checked the clock on the kitchen wall. Her voice

remained calm as she said, "I hope Jill hurries back inside. The guests must be about to finish their main courses."

"How can you remain so calm?" Mira asked.

Eve shrugged. As Mira had pointed out, Eve had tried to avoid William Hunter but he'd landed on her doorstep. Something... Someone was testing her. "I am not leaving this kitchen unattended," she said under her breath.

A few minutes later, Jill returned, her expression grim as she tucked her shirt in. She blew a lock of hair out of the way and announced in a resigned tone, "We have another guest. A late arrival."

Both Eve and Mira gaped at her.

"His car broke down," Jill explained, "And he walked the rest of the way, cutting through a lane. He missed his turn and ended up trying to climb over the hedge. That's when Josh and I tackled him to the ground."

"Isn't that a bit extreme, Jill?" Mira asked.

"Under the circumstances, no. I don't think so." Jill pushed out a breath. "Right... well... They must be finished by now, so I'm about to clear the table."

Mira's eyes widened slightly. "Who is the new arrival?"

"J.M. Kernel."

"The crime writer?" Mira's voice hitched with surprise.

Jill nodded. "He says he'll be happy with a cup of coffee and a whiskey."

Mira gave a pensive nod. "Oh, yes. I've heard rumors about his drinking. He must be between books."

Eve clapped her hands and drew their attention. "This is the home run, people. Let's make this happen and shove them out the door." Elsie McAllister was no doubt still hovering nearby, ready and waiting to witness something. Eve hoped she'd be satisfied with seeing the author being brought down by Jill and Josh. News would spread in no time and perhaps be embellished. By the end of the week, Eve knew the locals would be whispering about her chasing after J.M. Kernel with her sharpest knife. She could live with that.

"I'm beginning to find this very odd," Mira murmured.

"Unexpected guests arriving?"

"Yes. It's almost as if the universe is conspiring against you and taunting you."

"Well, it can taunt all it likes. I'm not taking the bait."

For the first time that day, Eve felt her mood lift, making her aware of how concerned she'd been during the last couple of days. Once the lunch guests left, she planned on enjoying a long, revitalizing soak in the bathtub in readiness for that night's dinner party.

They only had the coffee and dessert to get through.

Fingers crossed no one chokes on the coffee, Eve thought.

Chapter Four

IT TOOK Eve half an hour to talk herself into climbing out of the bathtub. All things considered, including the late arrivals, the intruders, and everything else that could have gone wrong but thankfully hadn't, lunch had been wonderfully uneventful.

Adjusting her pristine white chef's jacket, she looked in the mirror, her lips stretching into a wide smile. "You did great, Eve."

Instead of taking the back stairs down to the kitchen, she took the stairs leading to the front of the house. Now that all the wretched lunch guests had left, she would take a moment to enjoy her first official practice run. She would stride into her wonderfully cozy living room with the tiny rosebud wallpaper and antique furniture, and swirl around once, maybe twice, and do a victory dance to commemorate the moment.

Her dream come true, she thought. Her own inn in a small

island town inhabited by well-meaning people who would eventually, she hoped, come to appreciate everything she had to offer.

Halfway down the stairs, Eve heard the sound of voices drifting toward her. Her steps slowed. Had the evening guests arrived early?

She knew Mira's editor, Jordan, had planned on driving in early to have a business chat with Mira. Abby Larkin had been on the island since the morning catching up with friends. Eve expected her to arrive at about six, perhaps a little earlier to wander around the house that had once belonged to her.

Had she lost track of time? Checking her watch, Eve shook her head. Once she'd cleaned the kitchen, she'd given herself an entire hour to recover and prepare for that night's dinner. Again, she would remain behind the scenes. As much as she'd love to join her friends at the table, she really needed to get back into the swing of things and get used to preparing meals for others to enjoy.

A burst of laughter had her hurrying toward the sunroom. When she reached it, she stopped. There were two women she didn't recognize sitting on the floral couch and Elizabeth Rogue opposite them.

Why was she still here?

Backing away from the sunroom, Eve strode toward the kitchen. Along the way, she walked past the library only to double back. A man stood by one of the bookcases, his attention on a book he held. A woman sat in a corner, also reading a book.

Just how long had she been upstairs? After nearly dozing off in the bathtub, she'd decided to stretch out on the bed and close her eyes, but she could have sworn it had only been for a few minutes.

Jill hurried past her carrying a tray of drinks.

"Jill?"

"Not now, Eve."

Frowning, Eve strode into the kitchen where she found Mira deep in conversation with a man.

"Oh, there she is. Eve, this is Jordan Monroe. My editor."

Eve smiled and extended her hand. "Pleased to meet you." Turning to Mira, she asked, "Who are those people in the sunroom... and the library?"

"Oh, those are the stragglers," Mira gave her a brisk smile. "Remember J.M. Kernel's car broke down."

Eve gave a small nod.

"Well," Mira continued, "William and Stew Peters drove off with him to organize a towing service, so the others stayed behind. You know, the ex-wives, the editor, Julia Maeve, Marcus Leeds and Elizabeth Rogue." Mira waved her hand. "William should be back shortly to collect them."

"Why... Why did he leave them behind?" Eve exclaimed, her voice rising slightly, "They didn't all come in one car."

Mira gave a casual shrug. "They were reluctant to drive to William's house while he was out and about. So, they thought it would be easier to wait for him here. Don't worry about them. They've been well behaved. In fact, they've been so quiet I forgot all about them." Mira looked over Eve's shoulder. "Here's Abby."

Eve swung around. The previous owner of *Tinkerbelle's* Bookstore and the house Eve had turned into an inn laughed.

"You can't be surprised to see me because you were expecting me, so I have to assume Mr. Murphy has come knocking at your door."

Eve swung toward Mira. "There's another guest?"

"No, dear. I think Abby is referring to Murphy's Law."

Yes, how appropriate, Eve thought. She had planned everything so carefully and now, everything that could have gone wrong had gone wrong.

Eve scooped in a breath. Nothing had gone wrong. She couldn't lose her head over a slight delay. Soon, William would return and take his guests away.

Eve turned and smiled at Abby. "Great to see you. Would you like a tour of the house? I'm keen to know what you think about the renovations."

Abby grinned. "I came earlier than I'd planned so I've been poking my nose around for a bit now. Everything looks wonderful. I thought I'd feel nostalgic, but you've given the place a perfect face-lift. I love it."

Eve's relief surprised her. She only now realized she'd been on tenterhooks. Abby's house had been full of antiques and had aged with grace. While Eve had kept all the original decorative features, the heating and cooling services had been modernized, as well as the bathrooms. The pretty floral wallpapers had been toned down in the living areas, but she'd chosen bold colors for some of the bedrooms. "I think it might be too early for drinks. How about a coffee?" Eve offered.

"I wouldn't say no to an Irish coffee." Abby settled on a stool. "So this is your marvelous new bells and whistles French stove. I love the sea green color."

Eve was about to answer when Jill appeared.

Setting her tray down on the kitchen counter, Jill took a moment to gaze out the window. "I'm not sure how to break this to you, Eve. So, I'll just come straight out and say it."

Eve pressed the button on her other new toy, an Italian coffee maker, and told herself to remain calm. Nothing could be as bad as her unwanted lunch guests lingering.

"Martha Payne, the revolver carrying ex-wife who arrived late and likes to make a fuss, had a bit too much to drink and is now sleeping it off in one of the guest bedrooms."

Eve could feel everyone waiting for her response. She took her time adding a splash of Irish whiskey in Abby's coffee along with a dollop of freshly whipped cream. "That was very sensible of her. We wouldn't want anyone getting in their car after they've had one too many drinks."

"I've been plying her with coffee." Jill bit the edge of her lip and gave a tentative smile. "She should be good to go soon. William Hunter is back and he's rounding up the guests now."

Eve heard a collective sigh of relief.

Everyone began chatting at once.

Sinking down on a stool, Eve couldn't help laughing at the absurdity of the situation.

"You look relieved, Eve," Abby said.

"You don't know the half of it. I'm sure you'll hear all about it during dinner."

"Hear all about what?" Helena Flanders asked as she strode in, making up the fourth dinner guest.

"About how we all thought a lunch guest would be killed today," Mira offered.

Yes, an amusing tale, Eve thought, and it was now up to her dinner guests to make it through the night unscathed.

Helena laughed. "Well, I guess I made it just in time. It's looking quite threatening out there. So much for getting my hair done today. It's a mess. The wind whipped it all out of shape." Producing a bottle of champagne from her handbag, she handed it to Eve. "I know this is not the official opening, but we should still make a toast."

"Great idea," Mira said. "I'll get the champagne glasses."

The kitchen filled with lively chatter. Eve lapped it all up and even managed to put the horrible lunch experience behind her.

Helena strode around the kitchen counter and stood in front of Eve's new stove. "I feel I should kneel before it and pay homage. It's magnificent. I want one, but I'd have to knock down a few walls to make it fit into my kitchen."

Eve sniffed. "Is that cigar smoke I smell?" She turned to Jill.

"The men are all out on the front veranda," Helena offered. "As I was striding up the path, I saw William Hunter coming out of the house with a box of cigars under his arm."

Jill's mulish expression spoke of dire consequences. "He's supposed to be rounding up the guests."

Eve shook her head and surprised herself by saying, "Let's not antagonize them, Jill. They'll be out of our hair soon enough."

"I guess one of the windows is open," Jill said, "I'll go close it."

Abby gave Eve an encouraging pat on the back. "It won't be long now, Eve."

Before Eve could respond, a clap of thunder boomed right

overhead. The lights flickered but luckily came back on. Everyone spoke at once then the heavens opened up with rain pelting against the windows.

One by one, they all edged toward the windows to gaze at the deluge.

It took a good five minutes for the rain to ease up. As soon as it did, everyone launched into a lively conversation about the unwanted lunch guests.

Jill appeared and gave Eve a reassuring hug.

"Let me guess," Eve said, "Now they're going to wait for the rain to stop."

Jill gave a small nod. "It's nearly over. There's no need to panic."

"I have no reason to panic. This rain can't possibly last forever. Those clouds haven't stopped moving all day. It'll soon blow over." Eve drew in a hard breath. "If Martha Payne is too drunk to drive, she can hitch a ride with someone else and collect her car tomorrow." Eve gave a firm nod, thinking this was nothing but a kink in the road. "I'll get dinner started."

"Let's do the champagne toast first," Mira suggested.

"Good idea," Eve said,

"On the bright side," Mira said, "think of this rain as washing away everything that went on earlier today."

Yes, Eve liked the sound of that. A brand new start.

"I love the smell of rain," Abby remarked. "Right along with the smell of freshly laundered linen and new books."

Everyone concurred.

Mira nodded. "Nothing compares to the smell of a new book. The first time Eve saw me holding a book up and smelling it, she thought I had finally lost it, but then I caught her doing something similar while cooking risotto."

Eve gave them a dreamy smile. "The sizzling of the onions and rice when I add a splash of white wine always does it for me. It's magical."

Abby held her glass up. "I'm not sure it's actually appropriate to wish you luck, Eve. I get the feeling it would tempt fate."

"In my case, it would be taunting fate. Perhaps you could all quietly ponder your well wishes," Eve suggested. Smiling, she took a sip and sat back to enjoy the flow of conversation. After a good half hour, she set her glass down. "Okay. While you all enjoy yourselves, I'm going to get dinner started." She moved around the kitchen with a lightness to her steps she hadn't enjoyed in quite a while. She lost herself in the simple task of stirring and tasting. With everything falling into place for her, she even considered sitting down to enjoy dinner with her guests.

As she turned to smile at the tail end of a story, a piercing scream drowned out the chatter.

Everyone appeared to hold their breaths as if waiting for a prompt. Then, someone must have moved. From one moment to the next, they all rushed out of the kitchen and headed toward the front of the house.

Eve turned and gazed out at the window.

Hesitating, she hovered in an indecisive moment, feeling stuck between the devil and the deep blue stormy sea.

What now, she thought.

Martha Payne, the revolver carrying ex-wife #4, stood on the front veranda silently screaming. She had a bad case of pillow head, with one side flattened, while the other stood on end. She'd either succumbed to shock and had forgotten to close her mouth, or she was digging deep, trying to find her voice.

Eve guessed she had stirred awake and had then wandered downstairs.

The guests had formed a semicircle around Martha and stood gazing at the swing chair.

"I'd like everyone to please step back and give us some room."

Josh sounded in control of the situation but Eve knew she had to step forward and see for herself what the fates had dumped on her this time, literally, on her doorstep.

When she broke through the barricade of people, she stared, eyes unblinking at the man slumped on her swing chair, a cigar by his feet.

Josh gave a small shake of his head stating the worst even as he placed the 911 emergency phone call.

Without thinking, Eve bent down and picked up the cigar, setting it down on a saucer the guests had used as an ashtray. Briefly, she looked about her in dismay. Then she managed to speak, her voice strained around the edges, "Jill, could you get everyone inside, please?"

It took a moment for Jill to respond and herd the guests back inside. Not that it made a difference as they all found their way to the windows.

Eve scooped in a breath. "Josh, please check for a pulse again."

"It's no use, Eve." Josh straightened. "He's gone."

A gust of wind swirled around them. Eve shivered.

"You should go back inside too," Josh suggested.

As she turned, she heard sirens approaching, the sound drawing closer yet appearing to fade as it mingled with the wind and rain.

Inside, the guests' hushed tones filled the living room.

Eve felt helpless. Of all the places he could have died...

She raked her fingers through her hair.

Jill approached her. "You did the best you could, Eve. We took every precaution. No one could have foreseen this."

Had he been killed?

On her watch. In her brand new inn.

She'd be run off the island.

Eve brushed a hand across her brow. Should she start packing? Don't be ridiculous, she told herself. She had no reason to jump to conclusions. People died all the time, some from unexplained causes. Yes, that's it, she thought. Some people simply drew their last breaths and expired for no reason whatsoever. "I'll be in the kitchen." She could think there. She needed to collect her thoughts. Yes, that's what she'd do.

Jill gave her an encouraging pat on the shoulder. "I think that's probably for the best."

"What do you mean?" Eve didn't wait for Jill's answer. Looking over her shoulder, she saw the lunch guests had pinned their gazes on her. They weren't looking for guidance or explanations. Those stares were fixed on a single thought fired directly at her.

Guilty.

When Detective Jack Bradford strode into the kitchen, he found Eve in the middle of basting her roast quail. She returned the tray to the oven and turned her focus to peeling potatoes.

"Eve."

"Sorry, Jack. I can't stop. I'd prepared dinner for four. Now there are extra mouths to feed." She shrugged. "I assume they'll need time to recover from the shock. I can't have them waiting around on empty stomachs. Eating will give them something to do." She looked up. "Does that sound odd?"

"No. It's a natural response. You want to keep busy."

Eve turned a potato in her hand. "They think I had something to do with it, Jack."

"You're jumping to conclusions, Eve."

She chuckled under her breath. "You would too if you'd seen the way they looked at me. I swear I saw one of them take a step back."

"They're all in shock."

She set the potato down. "I should make sandwiches, not fries. Yes, that's what I'll do. Or maybe I should wait. They must be about ready to leave. After all, there's nothing for them to do now."

"Actually..." Jack looked anywhere but at Eve.

While she didn't wish to overreact, Jack's hesitation spoke of dire circumstances looming, gathering momentum and racing toward her.

"Jack, I don't really care for the sound of your tone."

Accepting the inevitable, she gestured with her hand. "Okay, let's hear it. I know you're holding something back."

He hitched his hands on his hips and met her gaze. "There's been some rain damage at the Hunter house. William Hunter just received a call from his housekeeper. Can you put them up for the night?"

She counted several heartbeats before responding, "Tell me you're kidding." She knew he wasn't and she shouldn't be surprised. Death always seemed to set unexpected events into motion, like a domino effect.

"Even if they could find somewhere else to stay, I would advice against any of them driving. One of the guests brought a case of whiskey he had in his car and they've been hitting the bottle," Jack explained.

"Whiskey? Who... Which one?"

Jack checked his notebook. "The author. J.M. Kernel. From what I understand, William Hunter and Stew Peters went out to organize a towing service. Is that right?"

"Yes."

"Well, J.M. Kernel had the whiskey in his car and he didn't want to leave it. When they returned from organizing the towing service, Jill told them another one of your lunch guests was sleeping if off, so they settled down on the veranda to smoke cigars and drink."

"You could give them a police escort," Eve suggested, "They can't be that far gone."

"And where do you suggest they go?"

She fished around for some ideas, but nothing came to mind.

Eve slammed her hands on the counter. "Well, shame on Roger McLain's cousin for selling William Hunter a leaky house."

Jack shifted slightly. "I'll be taking statements in the library. I'll do the Hunter guests first and then the others."

"The others?" She grabbed hold of a potato again as if that alone could ground her. Eve frowned. "Hang on. Aren't you supposed to wait until the coroner determines the cause of death before questioning people?"

Jack straightened. His face relaxed, taking on a pleasant blandness she recognized only too well.

"I'm only taking statements."

"You don't do that without a valid reason." She held his gaze for long seconds. "You suspect foul play."

Abby Larkin and Helena Flanders strode into the kitchen.

"All alone, Eve? If we'd known, we would have come sooner."

"Mira had been keeping me company to make sure I had an alibi at all times but now there's no more reason for that."

Both Abby and Helena stared at her.

"It's a long story. I believe you were going to hear all about it at dinner," Eve offered. "Did you give your statements?"

"Yes." Abby sat down on a stool. "I guess most of us had the same story to tell. We were all in here with you."

Eve tilted her head in thought. "But you arrived earlier and had a look around the house. Did you see anything unusual?"

"Nothing." Abby turned to Helena. "What about you?"

Helena nibbled on an olive. "I arrived just as William Hunter was coming out of the house with the cigar box under his arm, then I headed straight for the kitchen." Along the way, she'd also seen the same people Eve had seen in the sunroom and the library.

What were the chances of Jack being wrong?

Foul play?

He hadn't been specific, but if he'd noticed something suspicious, then he had to be on to something.

"I've never seen a corpse before." Abby shivered. "How many have you seen, Eve? You must have notched up quite a few by now."

Jill's appearance spared Eve the ordeal of having to answer.

"Well, I've given my statement," Jill said, "If there's a killer among us, I take my hat off to them because I've been run off my feet keeping an eye on everyone. I wish you'd gone ahead and installed security cameras in the common areas, Eve. It would make our job that much easier. Maybe now you'll give it some serious thought."

Eve stilled.

What on earth had she been thinking opening an inn? She might as well have issued open invitations. They'd joked about her inn becoming the ideal holiday destination for killers on vacation, but it hadn't occurred to them it might also become a murder hotspot.

No, not murder, Eve insisted. She couldn't afford to fuel Jack's suspicions. Or had they been her suspicions?

Her first dinner party at the inn. Ruined.

As for the victim...

She hoped he hadn't suffered.

Had he seen it coming? Had he felt something?

His family and friends would have to deal with the aftermath. No, she didn't want to think about it.

Helena smiled at her. "Cheer up, Eve. This makes it three deaths. You know what they say about disasters coming in threes. This should put an end to it all."

What if that became a recurring cycle of self-fulfilling prophecies? Eve sighed. "There's no reason to think this is murder."

"There must be a reason why Jack is taking statements," Jill said as she stood guard at the door, "Did he say anything to you, Eve?"

Eve shook her head. He might have said something more if she'd asked, but she hadn't. Jack had been right in telling her to avoid jumping to conclusions. Why worry about something until they had all the facts?

Eve gave a firm nod. As far as she was concerned, there was nothing wrong with hiding her head in the sand or finding refuge in peeling potatoes and making sandwiches.

Jill nibbled on the tip of her thumb. "Did he ask anyone about the cigar box? He wanted to know when I'd noticed it."

Eve stilled. Cigar box?

"Now that you mention it, yes," Abby chirped.

Helena picked up another olive. "Me too. I told him I saw William Hunter with it when I arrived."

"Cigar box?" Eve asked again. "Why would Jack ask about a cigar box?"

Jill shrugged. "Jack was annoyingly uncooperative. He flat

out refused to share any pertinent information. If there's something significant about the cigar box, then he's not saying."

Eve tried to think back to when she'd come down the stairs. She'd looked around but had she seen a box of cigars? "Jill, when you rushed by me in the hallway, you were carrying a tray of drinks. Who were they for?"

"I took those to the sunroom, for two of the wives, the newspaper editor, Julia Maeve and Elizabeth Rogue."

Eve had only noticed three women in the sunroom, including Elizabeth Rogue, the only one she recognized. Where had the other one been? Jill had delivered the drinks soon after Eve had poked her head in...

"I saw two people in the library," Eve said.

Jill nodded. "Miranda and her husband, Markus Leeds."

Eve set some glasses down on the counter and poured everyone some wine.

Jill curved her eyebrows. "Is that wise, Eve? You haven't given your statement yet."

About to answer, Eve looked up and saw Josh standing by the door.

"Eve." Josh gave her an apologetic smile. "Jack's ready for you now."

Eve shook her head. "I see. He's rounding up the usual suspects."

As she strode out of the kitchen, Jill patted her back. "You're a seasoned suspect, Eve. You've got this in the bag."

Chapter Five

EVE SETTLED down on the couch and, looking at Jack, she held up her hand, "Process of elimination. Information gathering. Following procedure. This isn't personal. I understand all that, Jack. No need to apologize. And, if you'd given me some warning, I would have brought you some coffee."

Jack looked down at his shoes and smiled. "I thought I did give you warning, Eve."

"And I thought you were joking."

"Does that mean I'm not getting coffee?"

Eve lifted her chin a notch. "I'm still processing the day's events. That means I'm still in shock and not functioning at full capacity."

"Really? I thought you and Jill had been expecting something to go wrong and taking necessary precautions." He flipped open his notebook. "Tell me about that, Eve."

Eve counted to three. "What happened here today defies all

logic." Eve sent her eyes dancing around the room. It seemed only yesterday that she'd sat here with Jack and had assured him they had everything under control. "You know as well as I do, I have been a victim of circumstances." Well beyond her control.

The edge of Jack's lip quirked up.

Eve waved her hand. "Being in the wrong place, at the wrong time. Comments I make being misconstrued. The list is endless. But, as you can see, I'm still guilt free. However, I appear to have been labeled a magnet for trouble and must therefore act accordingly to safeguard myself. Jill and I decided to play it safe. Despite everyone's efforts to keep me away from William Hunter, he came to me and he brought an entourage of people with him. I tried to dissuade his personal assistant from holding the lunch at the inn, but she insisted." Eve tilted her head, "Now that I think about it, she was determined to hold the lunch here. Have you interrogated her?"

"No one is being interrogated, Eve. I am merely collecting information while it's still fresh in people's minds."

Ignoring his comment, Eve said, "You should think about placing people."

Jack frowned. "What do you mean? You were all here, at the inn."

"Yes, but..." Eve shook her head and tried to get her thoughts in order. "We've been talking, Jill and I, and the others, trying to figure out if we'd seen anything out of the ordinary. Jill served drinks to four people in the sunroom, but shortly before she did, I poked my head in there and only saw three people."

"Which ones?"

"Elizabeth Rogue and two others. I don't know their names. I only know there were three and not four." She sighed. "I know it sounds like one of those complicated brain teasers. Three people climb onboard a train, which leaves the station at nine in the morning. At the next stop, one person gets off, while two get on." She waved her hand again. "You know what I mean."

"I'm almost afraid to say that I do," he murmured under his breath. Jack drew out a cell phone. "While Jill served lunch, she took some photos without anyone knowing. See if you recognize the other two people you saw in the sunroom."

"Jill took photos? She's definitely earned her keep."

Jack nodded. "Jill took caution to the extreme."

Even with the photos Eve had to think hard. She'd only seen the back of two of the women. Smiling, she tapped the screen. "These two." A woman with long blonde hair and a brunette with a short bob.

"Valentine and the editor, Julia Maeve." He checked his notebook. "Jill said she also served drinks to Liz Logan."

"As I said, I only saw three women. It was probably two or three minutes between the time I moved away from the sunroom and strode past the library where I bumped into Jill." In that time, Liz Logan had slipped back into the sunroom. Where had she been? Eve looked out the window. "The rain's eased up. Shouldn't William check on his house? He seems to be a man of action, taking off to rescue someone else's car. You'd think he'd be all over this, making sure any damage to his new house is minimized."

"I'm sure he'll get to it eventually." Jack cleared his throat. "Josh reported seeing a couple of people hovering around the inn."

"Nothing but locals preying on my vulnerabilities and hoping to catch me in the act."

Jack frowned. "Do you know who they were?"

Nodding, Eve told him about seeing Elsie McAllister. "I'm sure the other person belongs to her Sisters in Crime book club." She slid to the edge of her seat. "I'll have to go into damage control even before we're officially open for business."

"You'll be fine, Eve." Jack tapped his notebook. "You went upstairs straight after lunch."

"I see you're working on a timeline and, yes. I cleaned the kitchen and went upstairs."

"Did you stay up there until you came down?"

"Yes."

"Are you sure about that?"

"What are you getting at, Jack?"

"I'm following your suggestion and trying to establish everyone's whereabouts."

"Starting with me, the obvious suspect?" Eve shot to her feet. "Tell me about the cigars. Why have you been asking about them?"

"If we check your financials, are we likely to find you've purchased cigars?" Jack asked.

"Do I look like the type of person who buys expensive cigars?"

"What makes you think they were expensive?"

She assumed they were. After all, William drank expensive water, so it made sense that he also smoked expensive cigars. Eve crossed her arms and lifted her chin in defiance. "Are you brainstorming with me, Jack?"

"I might be."

"Since when?"

"Since you displayed an uncanny ability to stumble on information. Your unconventional methods seem to work for you."

She strode around in a tight circle. "You want to find out who is responsible for bringing the cigars here. I'm clearly the last person you've questioned, so no one else has come forth with information." She swung toward him. "Death by cigar?"

"Quite possibly. I'm not ruling anything out yet."

"Meaning..." her voice hitched, "He didn't die of natural causes?"

"It's too early to rule out suspicious circumstances. Either way, don't jump to conclusions, Eve," Jack warned.

Eve's eyes widened. "There is a killer staying at the inn?"

Jack sighed. "That's jumping to conclusions, Eve."

The moment Eve returned to the kitchen, everyone stopped talking and turned to her.

"Well?" Mira asked.

"Batten down the hatches. It's going to be a stormy night." Eve turned to Jill. "I think we should have dinner in the kitchen. The other guests can use the main dining room and living room."

Jill's eyes widened. "They're staying?"

Eve sighed. "William's house sprung a leak. We'll get them settled in. I think it would be a good idea to stay away from them. That means having dinner in the kitchen. I hope no one minds."

They all shook their heads.

"You can let Josh know he can come down from his lookout spot," Eve suggested.

"Oh, he abandoned that when he heard the scream. Now he's part of the investigation." Jill nodded. "I'm encouraging him to move up the rung and become a detective. I aim to be the woman who inspires him to greatness."

Eve gave her an approving smile.

"I've taken the liberty of pouring everyone drinks," Mira said.

Eve gave her aunt an easy smile. "Good thinking, Mira. Let's ply everyone with drinks and then hopefully, they'll all forget about today. Thank you."

Someone behind her cleared his throat. Eve turned and stared up at a mountain of a man. "Can I help you?"

He cleared his throat again. "I'd hate to be a pest. Is there any chance I might get a chunk of cheese and some bread? It's going to be a long night and there's really only so much drinking a person can do on an empty stomach."

"You must be the author," Eve said.

J.M. Kernel grinned. "At your service." He bent slightly at the waist and made a flourishing gesture with his hand.

Just what they needed, a happy drunk who no doubt could drink anyone under the table and do so while reciting poetry, or worse, singing.

"I'll organize some food shortly," Eve assured him.

"Thank you. I will be forever indebted to you."

Eve waited until he left before saying, "Huddle up, people.

We need to put our thinking caps on and try to remember if we saw anything unusual."

"What's this about, Eve?" Mira asked.

Eve spread her hands out. "Everyone please remain calm. There's no need for alarm."

Mira shook her head. "Eve, I prefer to make informed decisions. If I'm not going to panic, I need to know the reason why."

"This can't leave the kitchen." Eve signaled to everyone around her. "This is our circle of trust. Everyone else is persona non grata."

Mira frowned. "That's a rather serious statement to make about William Hunter and his guests."

"It's called comeuppance." Eve didn't see anything wrong with thinking they were all guilty until proven innocent.

"That's a rather harsh rebuke, considering the circumstances," Mira said.

Then why was Mira smiling? "I think you'll agree with me once I tell you..." Eve scooped in a breath and said, "The victim was killed by a cigar brought into my inn by an unidentified person. I'm sure Jack will soon find evidence to prove that." So much for taking a backseat, Eve thought.

"Killed?" Abby and Helena asked.

Eve gave a firm nod. "Jack denies it. He insists it's too early to call it murder. And while I wouldn't mind entertaining the possibility that this is nothing but an unfortunate case of death by natural causes, the odds are in favor of it being murder. While my sympathies go to the victim's family, I can't help thinking someone is clearly determined to burst my bubble of joy."

During the next half hour, everyone gave their own opinion about the box of cigars.

After hearing everyone's take on the situation, Eve realized her mistake. Now everyone's stories had merged and she couldn't tell what was what. No wonder Jack interviewed people individually.

Closing her eyes, she could actually see herself walking past the dining room and seeing the box of cigars. One moment, she saw the lid open and the next, closed.

She growled softly. "I suppose this is how evidence becomes contaminated."

Samantha strode in.

"You must be run off your feet, Samantha. Pull up a chair and have a drink," Eve offered, "By the way, can you remember seeing anyone carrying a box of cigars?"

Samantha tucked a stray lock of hair back and wavered. "Working in the bookstore, I'm used to paying attention. I've seen people become so absorbed with browsing, they forget they're holding a book in their hands and actually walk out without paying. Sorry to say I've found today a bit daunting. The women are all so glamorous, I felt out of my depth."

"You did a splendid job, Samantha. Don't worry about it. Something might come to you. Out of curiosity, did you notice the men at all?" Eve asked.

"Now that I think about it, no. They were in the background."

"What about you, Jill? By the way, Jack showed me some photos you took. Well done."

"Jack confiscated my cell phone," Jill grumbled. "As for the cigars... I'm sure I saw them."

"If we can have a look at the box of cigars, it might trigger people's memories," Eve reasoned.

Samantha shook her head. "I saw Detective Jack Bradford take it. It was an orange box. Give me a minute. Something about the label caught my attention. Oh, yes. The word dragon was on it."

Jill strode out of the kitchen and returned shortly with Eve's laptop computer. "Gurkha Black Dragon?" she asked after a quick search online.

"Yes," Samantha exclaimed.

"An orange box." Jill placed the laptop on the counter so that everyone could see the screen. "Yes, this is the one I saw. It's the *Black Dragon Special Edition Tubo*, the Rolls Royce of cigars and the brand's rarest and most unique, ultra-premium cigars."

They all leaned in and admired the orange box.

"Are we looking at the murder weapon?" Abby asked, her voice filled with awe.

Jill looked up from the laptop. "There has to be a reason why Jack asked us about it. So in answer to your question, yes, we are most likely, possibly... maybe, looking at the murder weapon."

They all took a step back.

Abby put her hand up. "Umm... You'll have to forgive me. This is all very unfamiliar to me. Does this mean someone brought that box of cigars to the inn with the intention of killing and, if so, who... and how?"

"Good questions, Abby." Eve strode around the counter and took her place behind the stove where everything felt safe. "I guess that's what Jack will try to find out."

Abby looked from one person to the other. "Meaning what?

Are we supposed to just wait? Hang on. If someone brought those cigars here, could the person still be here?"

"Don't worry, Abby. Eve and I are old hands at this," Jill assured her. "We'll have this figured out before dessert is served."

"We'll do no such thing," Eve warned. Belatedly, she regretted mentioning the cigars. As an innkeeper, it was her duty to ensure her guests' comfort. Instead, she'd raised the alarm, creating a hubbub over something they shouldn't concern themselves with.

Mira and her editor, Jordan, stood in the background, their attention still fixed on the laptop screen. They both shook their heads and took a couple of steps back as if trying to distance themselves from the whole situation.

Mira cleared her throat. "Would anyone else like another drink?"

Helena laughed. "I can't decide. Should I seek oblivion in a glass of wine or do I need to keep a clear head? Looking around, I think we're all assuming that box was brought in by one of the other guests." Helena turned to Jordan. "Who are you?"

Mira stepped in front of him. "He's my editor. Don't you dare suspect him. Good editors are as rare as hen's teeth." Mira turned to him. "Please don't prove me wrong... about you not being responsible for bringing the cigars, that is."

Abby stepped up to him and said in her soft tone, "He has been rather quiet."

Jordan Monroe gave Mira a nervous look.

"Okay, everyone." Eve put her hands up and called for calm. "Please leave Mira's editor alone. I can vouch for him." After all, he'd only come because Eve had insisted Mira needed to have a dinner party so that Eve could prove to the inhabitants of the town she was too busy to care about being excluded from their town meetings.

She set a platter of cheese on the counter. "Here's something to nibble on while I finish preparing dinner." Although she didn't think she'd be able to eat a bite. She turned her attention to preparing a platter of cheese and bread for the other guests. When she finished, she turned to Jill. "Are you game to go out there again?"

"Of course. It'll be the perfect opportunity to observe them. One of them might be a killer. It'd be great if I can figure out who before anyone else does."

"That's the spirit. Oh, and ask if anyone is interested in a steak."

Jill turned to the others. "Does anyone have a spare cell phone I can use to sneak some photos?"

Helena dug inside her bag. "Here, take mine."

Mira made the rounds topping up people's glasses. "It's strange. I had fixed in my mind the idea of William Hunter being murdered. Not that I really expected someone to kill him, or anyone else. Although, we must admit, Eve has set her own record for attracting murder and mayhem into her life. If there's a national average, I'm sure she's way ahead and in her own league. The odds were stacked against someone."

Eve lifted her glass in a salute. "Unique Eve. That's me." She looked up at the clock just as the minute hand hit the hour. The storm had eased up but hadn't moved too far. Outside, she could see a couple of police officers making the rounds. No one would come in and no one would leave without them noticing.

She didn't think Jack would leave her stranded in a house with a killer. It would be irresponsible. Yet... daring.

Eve distracted herself and the others by talking about the food she'd prepared and the wines she's selected, but even as she spoke and the others joined in the conversation, she could tell their hearts were not in it. Clearly because they would all prefer to be talking about the murder case.

The death, Eve corrected.

When Jill returned, everyone turned to her for news.

"J.M. Kernel is entertaining the guests with stories about the research he did for his latest book," Jill said, "I saw ex-wife #3, Miranda Leeds, on the verge of tears, but she recovered quickly. Her husband, Marcus, is sitting with a bottle of whiskey not far from his reach. The other ex-wives are all fretting. Valentine is pacing, but I think that has more to do with exercising her lunch off rather than worrying about the death. Liz Logan is biting her nails. Martha Payne is just sitting there staring into her wine glass. As far as I'm concerned, they are all acting suspiciously. I think the newspaper editor, Julia Maeve, is taking mental notes. Her eyes are everywhere. William Hunter is in the library with Elizabeth Rogue. I tried to eavesdrop on their conversation but they were whispering. Oh, and there are three people interested in steak." Jill poured herself a tall glass of water and drank deeply. "Spying is thirsty work." She held up Helena's cell phone. "I have some more pictures. If I can print them out, we could set up a suspect board and start generating ideas."

Everyone nodded and murmured their approval.

Mira put her hand on Jill's shoulder. "Don't you think that's a bit extreme? After all, the police are looking into the case. If, indeed, there is a case. For all we know, that man died of natural causes and Jack is only being overcautious and thorough."

Noticing everyone's attention shifting to the door, Eve swung around.

Jack stood by the door, raindrops trickling down his cheeks.

Eve sighed. "For heaven's sake. What now?"

"Eve. Could I have a word with you, please?"

Eve strode toward him with everyone else following her.

When she turned, they stopped.

She sighed. "I guess anything you have to say to me you can also say to them."

"I'm afraid it's not good news."

Eve turned to the others. "Is anyone here surprised to hear that?"

They all shook their heads.

Lowering his voice, Jack said, "The preliminary lab reports came in. All signs point to the possibility, and I can't stress that enough, it's still only a possibility, but considering our current situation," he raked his fingers through his hair, "The fact we're all housebound—"

Eve grumbled. "Stew Peters died of poisoning."

Chapter Six

"HOW COULD you drop a bombshell like that in front of every-one?" Eve asked in a hard whisper as she drew Jack into the kitchen and away from the door leading to the dining room.

Jack frowned. "I tried to be subtle, but you jumped to conclusions."

Glancing around her, Eve saw everyone agreeing with Jack.

"Was my conclusion wrong?" she asked.

Jack pressed his lips together.

"Well?" She knew he didn't want to come straight out and say it. So, she said it again. "You believe he was poisoned, but you won't know for certain until you get the lab results. Meanwhile, you would like us to take extra care. Thank you for giving me a few dots to join."

Jack looked almost relieved. Eve imagined he'd been in a difficult position. On the one hand, he wouldn't want to be an alarmist, but on the other hand, he had a duty of care and had to make sure they all survived the night.

The fact they were forced to spend the night together with a bunch of possible suspects still puzzled her. Deep down, she knew Jack would never deliberately put her in the path of danger.

"I know you want them all out of here, Eve—"

"Yes, yes. Finding alternative accommodation at such short notice, and on a stormy night, would be impossible, more so as my inn is the only place offering such services on the island."

Jack laughed under his breath. "They're putting their lives in your hands, Eve."

Frowning at his uncharacteristic behavior, Eve turned and sent her gaze bouncing from one person to the other. Everyone had leaned in to hear her murmured conversation with Jack. "Hands up anyone who instantly thought I had something to do with poisoning Stew Peters," she whispered.

Thinking they hadn't heard her, Eve was about to repeat herself when Jill's hand shot up.

"Jill!"

"What?" Jill whispered, "I'm not saying you did it deliberately. Maybe he had an allergic reaction to something he ate."

Eve closed the doors leading to the dining room. Knowing she'd need a buffer between the noise in her kitchen and the dining room, she'd had new doors installed. Fire-rated to avoid the spread of a disaster in her kitchen and just for good measure, double thickness to minimize the noise. She turned to face everyone. "There are other ways of ingesting poison."

Mira brushed her hand across her chin. "It's interesting that you should say that, Eve."

Eve turned to Jack. "Have you informed the others?"

He shook his head.

"Are any of them under suspicion?"

"We're still looking into it. At this point in time we don't have any proof to link back to any of them."

Eve brushed her hands across her face. "Jack, are you saying one of them is a killer but since you don't have enough proof to haul them away for further questioning, we are all going to spend the night under the same roof?"

Everyone stilled to hear Jack's response.

Eve knew he'd been placed in a difficult position. She could sense him trying to find the right words.

He cleared his throat. "I'll be here, along with some other officers," he offered.

Eve counted to ten, but her patience splintered. "Why can't you drive them away... somewhere."

"It's chaos out there, Eve. The storm has caused some damage. Emergency services are busy assisting. I'd prefer to contain the situation and keep everyone here."

Eve raked her fingers through her hair. "Wait a minute. This is unconscionable. The police would never deliberately endanger civilian lives." Either he didn't have enough information or he simply didn't suspect any of the guests.

"You have nothing to worry about, Eve," Jack assured her.

"That's what I thought when I allowed them to set foot inside my inn. Now the damage is done," her voice rose, "My reputation has been tarnished."

"In all fairness," Mira said, "Your reputation has never exactly been squeaky clean."

Eve looked at everyone around her and saw a mixture of shrugs and nods.

"You're all unbelievable." Eve turned to Jack. "I suppose you also expect me to feed you and your officers."

"If it's a problem, we could order takeout. Although, I'd rather not send one of my officers out there or have a delivery person driving in these conditions."

"And how long do you think it'll take for news about you getting takeout to spread? I can just imagine what everyone would say. The local police were so wary of Eve Lloyd's food, they ordered takeout." Eve lifted her chin. "I have a good mind to call your bluff. You can't possibly be serious about us all staying under the same roof." The firm set of his mouth said otherwise. Eve gave a small nod. "Fine. So, what do we do?"

"If anyone needs to leave this area, do so with a partner. Having said that, I don't believe you have reason to worry."

"In other words, we have no reason to worry but we shouldn't let our guards down." Jill rolled her eyes.

Resigned to this impossible situation, Eve sighed, "I assume the killer had a motive."

Jack nodded. "That's usually the case, but I didn't say Stew Peters had been murdered."

No, he hadn't. Eve tried to remember Jack's exact words but they'd meshed together with her impulsive conclusions.

Stew Peters had died of poisoning.

Regardless, Eve said, "You want us to believe it was personal and so the killer won't have reason to kill again. His job is done and now he's going to ride out this stormy night in the comfort of my inn. What if William Hunter and his guests suspect we're onto them?" Worse, what if the killer suspect...

"There's no reason why they should."

"Aha!" Jill pointed a finger at Jack. "You're not denying there's a killer among them."

Jack put his hands up as if to call for calm. "Have you allocated the rooms yet?"

Eve shook her head.

"I suggest you put them in the top floor. I'll have an officer standing guard on the landing. If anyone comes out of their rooms, they'll have to get past him. This should all be sorted out in the morning." He looked at her dinner guests. "I assume you're all staying the night?"

Mira grabbed hold of her editor. "I'll take my chances out there. I'm taking Jordan home with me. As intriguing as all this is, I'd rather not risk losing my editor."

Jack nodded. "If the weather conditions don't improve, I'll have to insist you all remain here."

"Let's hope it doesn't come to that." Helena raised her glass. "I'd love to stay, but I have an appointment early tomorrow morning. And Abby's staying with me."

That didn't surprise Eve. Abby had been hesitating about staying at the house she'd once owned saying she hadn't quite come to terms with the two murders that had taken place there.

Abby gave Eve a brisk smile. "Sorry, Eve. I'll stay for dinner, but I have no desire to become a statistic. Of course, I'll come by early tomorrow morning to see how you all fared."

"Hang on," Eve said, "If they're leaving, why can't the guests leave?"

"Because they have nowhere to go," Jill reminded her.

Eve tried to engage her brain. There had to be more options.

No, there weren't.

As the captain of this ship, Eve thought, she had no other option but to steer them all away from troubled waters or navigate them as best as she could.

Eve and Jill looked at each other. "I guess it's just you and me."

Jill nodded. "And the killer."

Eve washed her hands and checked her reflection on the bathroom mirror. "I can't believe I had to relieve myself with you standing guard."

Jill laughed. "You heard Jack. We have to travel in pairs. This reminds me of school. Hurry up. I want to go too."

Eve stepped out of the bathroom and nodded at the officer who'd also accompanied them. Once Jill emerged, he left.

"It's just the two of us now. Let's go have a peek at our killer guests," Jill suggested.

Along the way, they bumped into one of them.

"It's Valentine. The supermodel," Jill whispered.

"Can you please point me in the direction of the rest room?"

Clearly, the guests hadn't been given the same instruction to travel in pairs. Eve pointed her to the end of the hallway.

"This dreadful business has put me on edge," Valentine said as she swept past them.

Eve made a conscious effort to keep her eyes ahead but she

couldn't help turning and watching the woman walking away. "I don't think she ever stepped off the catwalk."

"Fancy walking like that in the middle of town. We'll have to try it someday. Hey, do you think she went in there to get rid of lunch?"

"Hang on, I'm actually trying to picture her as a killer," Eve said. "What do we know about Valentine?"

"Wife number one and soon to be wife number five. I've seen photos of her taking part in charity events and then there are the usual interviews reliving her glory days." Jill shrugged. "I'm a little intimidated by her. When she asked me for pink salt I swear she wanted to whip me for not bowing to her."

"Let's wait a moment. By the time she comes out, I might have thought of something to ask her."

Their patience paid off. When Valentine strode out of the rest room, she had her cell phone pressed to her ear. Seeing them, she disconnected the call.

She gave them both a raised eyebrow look.

Eve felt awkward hovering around.

"I love the wallpaper," Valentine said, and strode past them, her head held high.

"She's not the type to dirty her hands with murder," Eve murmured under her breath.

"No, but I think she might be the type to pay someone to do it for her. Let's nail her down with a solid motive."

"How are we going to find one stuck here for the night?" Eve asked.

"We'll use our collective memories. Someone must have

heard something or other. We only need a smidgen of information to paint a bright picture." Jill laughed under her breath.

"What's so funny?"

"I'm thinking of that TV show where a bunch of people are stranded on an island. The millionaire, his wife. The movie star. The professor and Mary Ann."

"Let me guess, they never got off the island?"

Jill nodded. "In every episode, their efforts to leave the island failed."

"Well, we have an advantage. We're in the kitchen with all sorts of knives. No one will dare make an attempt on our lives. Also, we have police presence. That should be enough to keep us safe."

They edged toward the living room.

"Let's just casually stand here for a moment."

As they watched the group, they saw Valentine move from one person to the other. She did all the talking while the others nodded.

"She's some sort of ringleader," Jill whispered, "I'm guessing she's telling them to hang tight. This will all be over soon. They are going to get away with it, so they have no reason to worry."

"You think they all had a hand in killing him?"

"It's going to be a long night. If we only have one suspect, we'll end up playing scrabble and Mira will beat us all hands down. I vote for keeping our minds otherwise engaged."

They both straightened and swung around only to collide with Jack who stood with his hands hitched on his hips.

"Lost your way?"

Eve stood her ground. "Keep an eye on the super model. I

mean, keep her in your radar but don't look at her. She's trouble. I can sense it."

"What are you basing your suspicion on?" Jack asked.

"She went to the rest room to make a phone call. That has to mean something. She could have been planning her getaway or alerting her accomplice."

"Because this is an inside job and she's been hired to kill everyone?"

Eve looked over her shoulder. "What if Stew Peters wasn't the only target?"

Chapter Seven

"THREE STEAKS with potato salad and sandwiches, just in case anyone wants to nibble on something and a basket with sandwiches and strong coffee for the police officers." As Jill took the plates into the dining room, Eve checked their table to make sure she'd set enough place settings for everyone. She hadn't planned on sitting down with them, but that was before her undesirable guests had taken over her living and dining rooms. Giving everyone a cheerful smile, Eve said, "I hope you haven't lost your appetites."

Everyone had settled around Mira who'd sat down with the laptop to, supposedly, do some research. They looked up and gave distracted nods.

Sighing, Eve checked on her quail. Seeing that it only had a few more minutes to go, she reheated the rosemary and red wine sauce she'd prepared earlier.

Jack came to stand beside her.

"Where's Josh?" Eve asked. "I want to know if he'll sit down to dinner or if he's happy with sandwiches."

"I'll let him know. He's hovering around the other guests. He's using his interest in J.M. Kernel's books as a cover. How are you holding up?"

Eve smiled. "Under the circumstances, as well as can be expected. Thank you for asking. I'm sure someday I'll be able to put a positive spin on this and have a good laugh about it."

Jack gave her a reassuring hug.

When they all settled down at the table, Mira cleared her throat. "I did some research online and hunted down a few gossipy articles about Martha Payne."

"The revolver carrying wife number four?" Eve asked. While she didn't want to encourage the conversation, the sooner they had a suspect, the sooner the group would be out of her inn.

Despite Jack insisting they had to wait until the lab reports came through, Eve was convinced Stew Peters had died of something other than natural causes.

"Yes, that's the one. They have one child. They're on good terms now, but they went through an acrimonious divorce. Martha dug up some dirt on him and won full custody of their daughter. Apparently, he'd been having an affair. They still have ongoing issues about her alimony, mostly concerning the fact William is quite generous when he wants to be, even after his divorces. Valentine, wife number one and about to become wife number five, received car upgrades every year while Martha had to make do with the same model Benz."

"That would give me reason for murder," Helena murmured. Having gone through a couple of marriages, she had a few tales to tell. "But William wasn't the target. Did Martha have any reasons to want Stew Peters dead?"

Jack sighed but refrained from once again reminding everyone the cause of death had yet to be determined.

Mira held up a finger. "Stew Peters is... was William's personal accountant and financial advisor."

Jill rubbed her hands. "Now we're getting somewhere. Maybe Stew Peters was responsible for tightening the purse strings and advising William against buying Martha Payne a new car."

They all looked at Jack.

"Guesswork will only get you so far," he offered.

"This wine sauce is superb, Eve," Helena remarked.

"Thank you. I'm glad to see everyone is enjoying the meal without fearing for their lives."

Abby grinned. "You should definitely have this on the menu."

"I'm thinking of doing game dishes on Sundays. Jill thinks I should have fun food on Friday nights. Burgers and pizza. I'm also thinking of having guest chefs, perhaps once a month. But that depends on how fast word spreads about my Inn of Death. The idea might never see the light of day."

A hard thump had them all looking up and turning toward the dining room. After a couple of minutes of silence, they resumed eating.

"More wine anyone?" Eve offered. As she topped up everyone's glasses, she gauged their moods. So far, she didn't detect anyone on edge and eager to leave.

Jack put his hand over his glass. "None for me thanks."

"That's very conscientious, Jack. Do you think Josh could give Jordan and me a lift home?" Mira asked.

"Of course."

"Then that's settled. I'll have another glass, Eve."

The meal proceeded in silence until Eve asked, "How is everyone doing?"

Mira smiled. "Food is a great pacifier, Eve. As is wine."

Another hard thump, this time followed by quick footsteps, had them all looking around again.

Jack sighed. "I suppose I should go see what that's about."

"Didn't you say Josh is with them?" Eve asked. "If something's happened, then surely he'd either call for help or... Yes, I suppose it'd be better if you went to see. For all we know, William's guests have turned on Josh and are going to use him as leverage for their immediate release."

Jack was already out the kitchen door as he said, "No one is being held against their will."

When he returned, he shook his head. "Marcus Leeds had one too many glasses of whiskey. His wife made an attempt to put the bottle out of his reach, but that only made him get up and stumble his way to it."

"Are you sure he's drunk?" Eve asked. "He might be faking it. You know, filling his glass and, when no one is looking, tipping the contents into one of my pot plants."

"Why do you think he'd fake getting drunk?" Jill asked.

Eve shrugged. "To avoid detection. If a killer is hiding in that group, I'm thinking he wants to keep a clear head, and listen to everything everyone says to make sure no one is onto him. I'd hate to see one of my plants suffer because someone is trying to get away with murder."

Jack smiled. "Marcus Leeds is actually sitting by the window, Eve. I didn't see any plants near him. And, for the record, I'd agree with your theory about the killer trying to fly under the radar by appearing to be drunk."

"Jack. This must be the first time you've agreed with me." Eve raised her glass in a toast. She also noticed he hadn't discouraged her from stoking that particular fire of suspicion.

One of the guests... a killer.

Lowering his voice, Jack said, "Let's try to contain the situation, Eve. Keep everyone here and avoid the guests." Jack focused on finishing his meal. When he did, he excused himself. "Excellent meal, as always, Eve. I promised Josh I'd relieve him of his duties so he can sit down to dinner."

Jill rubbed her hands. "Great. We can get a fresh perspective."

Everyone gave Josh enough time to at least get halfway through his meal before asking him for updates.

"Jack thought we'd have trouble keeping the guests here, but none of them are fit to drive," he said, "J.M. Kernel is entertaining them with stories. He appears to be slurring his speech, but I swear I haven't seen him refill his glass."

Eve and Jill exchanged a knowing look. They both turned to Mira. "Do you know of any connection between the author and Stew Peters?"

Mira nodded. "All the people in there belong to William Hunter's social set. They spend weekends together. They even travel together. William Hunter has a yacht. When he vacations in the Caribbean, he takes them along."

Eve took a sip of wine. "That would have been a perfect place to kill Stew Peters. Why choose my inn, especially on a stormy night like this?" She waited for someone to suggest her reputation would make the inn a convenient setting. Surprisingly, no one did. "Josh, do you know what William and Elizabeth were talking about? Jill said she saw them in the library."

"Funeral arrangements," Josh offered, "Stew Peters didn't have any close family so William is organizing it all."

"He's not such a bad sort," Helena remarked.

William Hunter the Third. Generous host. Generous husband, when he wanted to be. Generous friend. Give the man a halo, Eve thought.

Jill grinned. "I wonder what William is hiding? Maybe he wants to bury the evidence as soon as possible."

Eve hid her smile and wondered if William would have reason to want Stew Peters dead.

The cruise trip she'd recently gone on with her aunt had been reported on the Bugle. It had caught William's interest and had compelled him to buy the small town newspaper. Why? Had he seen an opportunity he could take advantage of? Eve shook her head. Being suspicious of someone didn't always pave the way to discovering a motive for murder. Looking up, she noticed Jill studying her.

"What?" Eve mouthed.

"Nothing," Jill mouthed back and then turned to everyone at the table. "Does anyone know anything about poisons?"

Abby cleared her throat. "Why do we think he was poisoned?"

They all looked at each other.

Eve poured some more wine. "It's nothing but an assumption, Abby. One we're happy to play around with."

Josh said, "J.M. Kernel must know a lot about poisons. He's used them in several of his books. They're his weapon of choice."

"Since Jack made a point of asking about the box of cigars," Jill said, "We have to assume he suspects they were used to deliver the poison. Perhaps they were laced with arsenic."

Shock registered in everyone's faces as they all looked at Jill. Anyone would think Jill had just announced the identity of the killer.

"Jill, we're not even sure it was poison. I won't be convinced this is the work of a killer until I see someone being hauled away in handcuffs." A small part of her wished, with all her heart, this had all been a silly mistake. A bigger part of her hoped Stew Peters had died of natural causes. Eve nudged Josh. "Can you back me up, please?"

Josh cleared his throat. "Well, as a matter of fact—"

Grinning, Jill said, "See, I told you."

"Let the man finish. Josh, you were going to say something. Why did Jack suggest Stew Peters had died of poisoning?"

"Actually," Jill said, "I think you're the one who mentioned poison, Eve."

Yes, she had. Mouthing an apology, she resumed eating.

"The test results haven't all come in yet," Josh said, "However, I noticed the bluish discoloration around the lips. That could be a sign of poisoning."

Jill clapped her hands. "Now we have to figure out which poison the killer used."

"Assuming the killer used a cigar as a weapon," Eve said, "It would have to be something that wouldn't be easily detected."

Abby Larkin drained her glass. "Is this what normally goes on between you two?"

Jill nodded. "We always try to stay out of police business, but then we can't help ourselves. Two heads are better than an entire police force and Eve and I have always managed to offer a fresh spin on theories." Jill grinned. "So far, we have a one hundred percent success rate."

Eve sighed. "I'm only going with the flow and making conversation. The police have this under control. This time, I am determined to stay right out of the investigation."

Mira chortled. "You always say that, Eve. And then you end up right in the thick of it."

Eve rose to her feet. "This time it's different. I really can't afford to meddle. With the inn opening so soon, I just don't have the time." She collected some plates and strode over to the kitchen.

Jill followed her and helped Eve stack the dishes in the dishwasher. "Getting back to what I was saying before. I've had second thoughts. Poisoning the cigars wouldn't make sense. William and J.M Kernel smoked cigars too, but only Stew died."

Jill gaped. "Hang on. I've changed my mind again. What if only one of the cigars had poison in it?"

"You think someone played Russian roulette?" Eve asked.

Jill gave a vigorous nod. "Yes. The killer laced one cigar with poison. Then he gave William the box thinking they could watch him enjoy his way toward the poisoned one."

"That means the killer wanted to bide his time." Eve brought out the coffee cups and set them on the counter. "I think we can safely assume it's someone close to him. Someone he sees regularly. The killer would watch him lighting up and wonder if today would be his lucky day. The killer's lucky day, not William's."

"But that means the killer didn't expect William to share the cigars," Jill offered.

"We need to find out if William is a regular cigar smoker and how he feels about this particular brand. Maybe he has different types of cigars. Those only he smokes and the ones he shares with friends." Eve looked up and smiled. "Cake and ice-cream anyone?"

Everyone stared at both Eve and Jill, mouths gaping open. Finally, they all nodded.

Eve held up a hand. "Yes, yes. I know. I can imagine what you're all thinking. I said I wanted nothing to do with any of this and I promise I will stay out of this investigation. Jill and I are only tossing around ideas."

Jill nodded. "We're just making conversation. While we should wait for Jack to reveal more information about the cigars, there's nothing wrong with prodding around. For instance, we can't really assume only one cigar has been poisoned."

Eve frowned. "That would be too macabre. But if we're right, it does tell us something about the killer. He... or she is patient and likes to play games."

"I've heard say poison is a woman's preferred weapon." Jill took the laptop and settled down at the table. "I'm going to research poisons. One way or another, we'll get to the bottom of this. Unless, of course, someone wants to talk about something else." She looked around the table.

Everyone shrugged.

Josh cleared his throat. "Actually, guns remain everyone's weapon of choice. Followed by knives."

"Really? Let me see." Jill did another search. "Oh, yes. You're right, Josh. However, poison remains more popular among women killers than among men."

"There you go," Mira piped in, "You learn something new every day."

By the time they'd had their coffee and dessert, everyone had agreed arsenic seemed to be the most likely poison used.

"Just think about it," Helena said, "you'd only need to dab the tip of the cigar with poison."

"It sounds feasible," Abby agreed, "But where does one get arsenic from?"

Eve smiled. "As no one seems to know, I believe the immediate population can feel safe in their homes. Clearly, it's not something one can easily get their hands on." Eve finished her coffee and set her cup down. She tried remaining silent, but the words pushed their way out, "How long were the men out on the veranda smoking?"

"I'd say about an hour," Jill offered.

"So we're looking for a fast acting poison."

Jill tapped away on the keyboard. "That could be anything, but the dosage would have to have been strong. If Stew Peters had a heart condition, the poison might have come from the foxglove plant."

"How would you extract the poison and how would you put it in a cigar?" Eve wondered.

"Where there's a will, there's a way," Mira offered.

Jill hummed. "I'm keen to find out more about J.M. Kernel's knowledge of poisons. Josh, can you think of any specific examples from his books?"

Mira shook her head. "It can't be him. He had a cigar too."

"But if he's the killer," Jill reasoned, "He would have known which cigar to take and which one to avoid. Let's assume, for the sake of brainstorming, he wanted to kill Stew Peters. We should find out how the cigars were offered around. Maybe J.M. Kernel simply picked one up and gave it to Stew. Confident he'd delivered the fatal cigar, he would then have passed the box around."

Thinking she'd already said enough, Eve pressed a glass of water to her lips. She desperately wanted to avoid being drawn into the conversation but, in her effort, she nearly choked on the water she drank. "If the cigars were given to William, why would J.M. Kernel offer them around?"

"Because they're a big happy family without boundaries," Jill chirped. "Oh, and that opens a can of wiggly worms. What if that's not all they shared?"

"Where is your mind going now?" Eve asked.

"I'm thinking about crimes of passion and revenge."

Eve smiled. "And I think you're being fanciful."

"Hey, it's a stormy night and I'm trying to liven the conversation."

Helena raised her glass in a salute. "And you're doing a splendid job of it, Jill. I doubt I'll be able to get any sleep tonight. My mind is buzzing with ideas."

Jill straightened and looked at Eve. "See, they're interested in my theories."

"Can I interest anyone in more coffee and perhaps some cognac?" Eve set a dish of chocolate truffles on the table. "These are brandy truffles."

Helena helped herself to a chocolate. "Abby's driving so I'll say yes to everything."

Eve looked toward the dining room. "I suppose I should offer the other guests some coffee."

Jill joined Eve in the kitchen. "I'll help with the coffee."

"You mean, you'll supervise and make sure I don't slip something in the drinks."

"I wouldn't want anyone pointing the finger of suspicion at you. The night is still young, leaving plenty of time for someone else to be murdered."

A clap of thunder had them all tensing.

"I'll go relieve Jack. Thanks for dinner, Eve." Josh grabbed a couple of chocolates and left.

Moments later, Jack appeared. "Josh tells me you've come up with some interesting ideas."

"It's nothing more than lively dinner conversation," Eve said.

"Eve is being modest," Jill laughed. "I think we'll have the case solved before the end of the night. Abby made an interesting point earlier." Jill gave a small nod. "If I had to buy arsenic, I wouldn't know where to start looking. That's why I'm in favor of some sort of plant. Even tomato plants are poisonous."

Mira's editor cleared his throat. "Ricin is a possibility. With adequate instructions and some knowhow, it could be produced."

Eve looked at Jordan Monroe. He'd been joining in the conversation but he'd mostly been listening. While she wouldn't readily voice her opinion, a part of her couldn't help thinking he would be the perfect killer. No one suspected him. On the surface, he didn't have any connection to the victim or any reason to kill him. That, however, didn't exclude him from committing a random murder.

Jill stilled. "Ricin. I've never heard of that one."

"It's highly toxic," Jordan offered.

"Great." Jill rubbed her hands. "How do I get some?"

Jordan smiled. "It's produced from castor oil seeds. A dose of purified ricin powder, the size of a few grains of table salt can kill an adult."

Jill's eyes sparkled with excitement. "And what's the most effective way of using it?"

Jordan exchanged a look with Mira. "Inhalation."

Jill jumped on the spot. "Aha! If I wanted to kill someone using a cigar, I could..." She tapped her finger on her chin. "I could make a tiny incision in the cigar and insert the ricin."

Eve shook her head. "The first puff would be enough for smoke to come out of the hole. A smoker would be instantly on the alert."

Everyone turned to Jordan. He shrugged. "If we're talking about a small hole, you could cover it with some superglue."

Jill smiled at Mira. "I can see why you're so protective of your editor. He is a fount of knowledge."

Nibbling on a chocolate, Eve said, "So back to motive. Why would someone want to kill Stew Peters?"

"What if he wasn't really the target?" Jordan asked.

Mira gave him a pat on the back. "Now you're just winding them up. They'll be at it all night."

Eve growled softly under her breath. "I really don't like the sound of that because it means someone wanted to commit murder in my inn and didn't particularly care who got killed. In a roundabout way, that would make me a target too, but since I've never met William's friends, I haven't given them a reason to involve me in a crime." Eve jumped to her feet. "I'd like to know how those cigars got here."

"Either one of the guests brought the box of cigars or someone delivered it to the inn." Jill threw her hands in the air. "That's it. The water was delivered this morning. The police need to question the delivery person. Maybe they're responsible for also delivering the deadly weapon."

Both Jill and Eve turned to Jack.

Jack gave a slow shake of his head. "I wish someone had mentioned this earlier."

Eve lifted her chin slightly. "I think I might have, but you seem determined to do everything you can to keep me out of the loop, and that includes not listening to me."

Jack appeared to be calling for calm. "Do you remember the name of the delivery company, Eve?"

"No. I didn't have to pay for the water. It came with a note explaining William only drank that particular brand of water. I assumed Elizabeth Rogue had organized it all and gave instructions to include the note. I'm not even sure if I kept it. I'll have a look through the trash here. You can search the trash outside." She looked out the window. "Although, with this weather you might have to wait until morning."

Jack was already on his feet. "Any leads will help. Perhaps the note was written on company paper."

He could also ask Elizabeth Rogue. The fact he didn't mention it made Eve wonder if perhaps he wanted to keep a close eye on the guests without giving anything away, at least while they were all sequestered at the inn.

"What about the whiskey?" Jordan asked. "It would be easier to lace a glass with poison."

Mira nudged Jordan. "You're getting into the spirit of it, but we should get going now. Otherwise I might have to drag you away. Besides, I can see another thunderstorm heading our way and I'd rather not get caught in the middle of it, or worse, be stuck here for the night. There's only so much excitement I can take."

Jill sipped her coffee. "Jordan makes a good point. We should widen our net and stop fixating about the cigars."

"Jill, I think you've had enough coffee." Eve tried to take the cup from her but Jill held onto it.

"I have no intention of sleeping tonight. Hey, didn't J.M. Kernel bring the whiskey? My finger of suspicion is itching to point in his direction."

"Put your finger away. They are all still guests and we must remain unbiased." Eve cleared away the remaining cups and stacked them in the dishwasher.

Mira and Jordan wished everyone a good night. "I'm only a phone call away, Eve. Call if anything happens."

Helena and Abby both got up too. "We might as well follow. I don't really look forward to being on the road in this weather. Thank you for the wonderful meal and entertainment, Eve. This is one dinner party I won't forget any time soon."

Eve turned to Samantha. "If you're not staying, you should leave now and get a police escort home."

"I hope you don't mind, I'd rather leave tonight." Samantha hurried after them.

After showing them out, Jill and Eve returned to clean up the kitchen.

Jill yawned. "And then there were two."

"Two plus nine guests and the police. I suppose we should go up and make sure all the rooms are in order," Eve suggested.

"Do you think the guests would agree to being handcuffed to their beds for the night?" Jill asked, "It would make our lives that much easier."

Eve snorted. "Think about it, Jill. They've spent the night eating and drinking. Do you really think it would be a good idea to handcuff them?"

"It was just a thought. I guess I can't quite picture Jack agreeing to it. He'd want proof of guilt."

Eve grinned. "Also, I'm sure it's against the law to hold someone against their will, not to mention tying them up. I might end up with a lawsuit on my hands." Halfway up the stairs she wondered if she had grounds to sue William Hunter.

Then another thought occurred. She could sue the entire town for libel and name Roger McLain as the instigator.

When they reached the landing, Jill grabbed hold of her arm. "Did you see that?" She pointed to the end of the hallway. "Someone just slipped inside one of the bedrooms."

No one was supposed to be up here yet.

Chapter Eight

"WHAT ARE YOU DOING?" Eve whispered and tugged Jill back.

"This is our chance to catch the killer in the act."

"What killer?" Eve pulled harder. "We need to get Jack."

"You've lost your touch, Eve. What's come over you? Where's the fierce Eve I know who would jump at the chance to confront a would-be killer?"

"That Eve only comes out when there are no options but to fly into the face of danger. The Eve standing beside you has no desire to be reckless. We have police officers hovering around the place. Let them do their job. And stop pulling back. This isn't a tug of war. We need to be sensible."

"I can't believe we're going to argue about this." Jill gritted her teeth. "We're going in there, even if I have to drag you kicking and screaming."

When Jill pulled, Eve dug her heels in only to find herself being dragged along the hallway.

"Are you out of your mind, Jill?" Eve asked in a hard whisper. "I didn't want to say anything, but now you've forced my hand. I'm worried about you. Ever since I told you about William Hunter's lunch, you've been acting strangely."

"Do you blame me?" Grunting, Jill dragged her along another couple of inches.

A hard thump had them both holding their breaths and straining to hear more.

"What if there are two people in there and one is being murdered right now?" Jill whispered. "There's no time to go down and get Jack and if we scream out his name, we'll alert the killer."

"That actually sounds like a good plan. If we scream, the killer will stop in his tracks." Eve shook her head. "Just listen to me. Now I sound as crazy as you." When had everything begun spiraling out of control? Everything had been going supremely well for her. And then William Hunter had shown up and her time to shine and revel in her new venture had been snuffed out... "Okay, so what's the plan?" Eve asked.

"We'll use the element of surprise and burst in," Jill said, "That way, we get to witness the act and have proof of his guilt. We don't want him getting off on a technicality."

"Such as?" Eve asked, her tone cautious.

Jill shrugged. "He might say he was trying to pull the knife out, not push it in."

He? "Hang on. What knife?"

"The knife. The murder weapon. Whatever."

Eve gave a reluctant nod.

"On the count of three," Jill said as she curled her fingers around the doorknob. They both mouthed the count and when they reached three, Jill flung the door open and flipped the light switch on.

A woman sprung up on the bed. Her piercing scream had both Eve and Jill jumping back.

"Happy now?" Eve asked. "It's just one of the guests having a lie down."

The woman continued screaming. Within seconds Eve heard hurried steps storming up the stairs. "I hope you have a ready explanation. That's Jack coming up." Eve considered trying to calm the woman down. Instead, she backed away from the bedroom.

"What's going on?" Jack asked as he approached them.

Eve waved her hand and calmly said, "False alarm, Jack."

Jack came to stand beside Eve at the door. "What did you do to her? Why is she still screaming?"

"We didn't do anything." Eve gave a casual shrug. "We... We just scared the living daylights out of her."

"It's Martha Payne." Jill turned to Eve. "The revolver carrying wife #4."

And a natural born screamer.

She must have been dreadfully noisy as a baby.

Recovering, Martha Payne demanded, "What do you mean by barging into my room?"

"We saw you skulking about," Jill offered, her tone accusatory. "We thought you might be the killer. You can hardly blame us. No one is supposed to be up here. We haven't assigned the rooms yet."

Martha threw a pillow at Jill. "I wasn't skulking."

"We saw you sneaking about," Jill insisted and threw the pillow back.

Eve noticed Martha Payne hadn't bothered defending herself against the ludicrous accusation that she might be the killer. In fact, she hadn't even blinked at the mention of a killer. Even if she'd had one too many drinks, surely, she should have shown signs of concern.

"I came upstairs and walked into a room with the most horrible striped wallpaper," Martha complained, "It made my head spin and my stomach turn, so I decided to find a less ghastly room."

Eve's mouth gaped open. The striped wallpaper had cost her a small fortune. She'd spent hours going through swatches to choose the perfect Art Deco replica.

Jill lifted her chin. "You say that now. How do we know you didn't plant some sort of murderous device in the other room?"

"That's thinking on your feet, Jill," Eve murmured.

Jack shook his head. "I can see you have this under control. If you need me, I'll be downstairs."

Eve grabbed hold of him. "Jack. Don't you dare leave."

"This is a housekeeping matter, Eve."

"What about Jill's suspicions," Eve asked, "Jill's right. Martha Payne might have been planting some sort of trap for another unsuspecting victim."

Jack raked his fingers through his hair. "It's the end of a long day for you, Eve. Let's not get carried away."

"It's not so far-fetched." Eve turned to Jill. "Tell him."

Jill backed away from the bedroom and closed the door. "Well, some poisons can be absorbed through the skin. How do we know Martha didn't smear some on the bed linens? Think about it. If I'd been drinking and looking for a bed to crash in, I'd head for the first door. Instead, Martha Payne went to the end of the hallway. That doesn't make sense to me. Tell me you see something suspicious in that action."

"Jill has a point," Eve nodded. "Although, being drunk, maybe Martha Payne simply overshot her aim and stumbled her way to the end of the hallway."

"I'll have a look," Jack said, "Will that make you happy?"

Eve thought about it for a moment. "Actually, locking her bedroom door would please me no end."

"You really think she was up to no good," Jack said.

Jill crossed her arms. "We saw her coming out of the next room."

Eve didn't contradict Jill. In reality, Eve had only seen a shadow disappearing into the bedroom.

Shaking his head, Jack strode to the next room. "Is this the one?"

"Yes," Jill said and followed him, leaving Eve no choice but to follow.

"Nothing appears to have been disturbed," he said.

Jill strode up to the bed and pulled back the covers.

Jack chortled. "What exactly do you hope to find?"

"I've been reading about poisons. Do you know people died from arsenic poison absorbed from their clothing? Clothing in the nineteenth century was so thoroughly dangerous it's amazing anyone survived. Arsenic was used to achieve a popular emerald green color used on dresses and ornaments. People got sick and died."

"Are you suggesting Martha Payne spread arsenic on the bed linen?" he asked.

"It's possible."

"But Eve didn't assign the rooms yet. No one knows who's getting which room," Jack reasoned.

Jill lifted her chin. "Martha might be on a killing spree. Out to get anyone and everyone. She might have sprinkled some sort of deadly dust on the pillows. Perhaps the same deadly substance she inserted inside the cigar."

Jack looked around the room. "And now she's taking a well-earned rest before she strikes again?"

"Is he mocking us?" Jill asked.

Eve put her arm around Jill's shoulder. "Best to let it go, Jill. I want all the guests in their rooms with a police officer at the end of the hall to make sure they all stay in their rooms. It's the only way I'll get any sleep tonight."

"Really, Eve? What if I'm right?" Jill insisted.

Eve sighed. "Jack. Is there any way we can check to make sure the linen hasn't been tampered with?"

"Or the soap," Jill exclaimed, "The possibilities are endless. It's up to you if you want to take this seriously or risk having another murder to investigate."

Jack chuckled under his breath. "You're about to suggest I get the CSI team in here to test all surfaces for poisonous substances."

Jill pressed her lips together and shrugged. "Better safe than sorry."

Eve looked over her shoulder. All this time they'd been upstairs, the kitchen had been left unattended. "Oh, hell. You two do what you have to do. I'm going down to my kitchen. There's no telling what might have happened in the time I've been up here."

"Eve, remember what I said about pairing up," Jack warned.

Jill huffed out a breath. "Fine. I'll go down too, but if you find anything, I want to be the first to know about it."

Eve tucked back her hair. "I've no idea how we're going to do this. I can't be in two places at once. How could I have dropped my guard?"

"Don't beat yourself up about it, Eve."

"I left the kitchen unattended." Eve stopped at the door and peered inside the kitchen. "Coast is clear." Yet she couldn't shake off the feeling anything might have happened during those few minutes they'd been upstairs.

"I'm going to go check on the guests," Jill said, "Josh should be there. He'll know if anyone left the living room."

Eve began wiping down surfaces, all the while checking to see if she could see anything out of place.

When Jill strode back in, her eyes sparkled with amusement. "You can breathe easy. Josh assures me no one, except Martha Payne, left the living room and he didn't take his eyes off anyone."

"That's a relief." Eve stood in the middle of the kitchen and slowly turned around. "I'm going to have to spend the night here. What was that poison Jordan mentioned?"

"Ricin. That's a really potent one. You only need a few grains of it to kill someone."

"Could it be mixed in with things like sugar and coffee?"

Jill gave a pensive nod. "Okay. At this rate, we'll never eat anything that comes out of this kitchen. Just as well Josh didn't leave his post."

And yet...

Eve slumped down on a chair. "I've got a bad feeling about this."

"Sorry." Jill paced around the kitchen. "You seem to have caught my bug. I can't remember ever being so suspicious of everyone. And now that I think about it, Mira's editor seemed to be very knowledgeable about poisons. Did he ever come anywhere near the kitchen?"

"As far as I know, he was always on the other side of the counter." Eve shook her head. "What am I saying? Mira's editor would have no reason to kill."

"You're right. We are getting a bit carried away. Come on. I told Josh we need to go upstairs to check the rooms and that he's not to let anyone out of his sight."

Half an hour later, they returned to the kitchen and found a police officer standing guard at the door.

"Thank you." Eve offered him a coffee. "You can let the guests know their rooms are ready. They can have whichever one they want."

"They're in no hurry to turn in for the night," Josh said as he relieved the officer from his post.

Eve checked the clock. "It's nearly midnight. Are they going to hold an all-night wake?"

Josh nodded. "Looks like it. I think we'll all need more coffee. I should get back to my post."

While Eve prepared the coffee, Jill sat down at the table and did some more online searching. "I want to find everything I can about our guests. I've created a document listing everyone's names," Jill said as Jack joined them. "Well?" she asked him, "Did you find anything?"

He shook his head. "Nothing looks to be out of place."

"Nothing you could see," Jill murmured under her breath. "As I was saying... What was I saying? Oh, yes... I suppose the police will be looking into everyone's finances. Someone purchased those expensive cigars and there has to be a trail leading back to them. They cost too much to have been purchased with cash."

"We still need to come up with a motive." Eve handed Jack a mug of coffee. "As William's advisor, Stew Peters might have been influential enough to put him in someone's crosshairs. We might have to mingle with the guests and see if we can prod something out of them."

"What happened to staying out of it, Eve?" Jack sipped his coffee and murmured his appreciation.

"I'm only talking so I don't fall asleep. They will all be gone by tomorrow." She held Jack's gaze until he nodded. "Okay. Now I'm worried because that was a half-hearted nod."

"I can't offer any assurances they'll be out of here tomorrow. It all depends on the damage at William Hunter's house."

"I swear I will skewer Roger McLain. He practically announced to everyone at the town meeting I'd somehow be responsible for ruining his precious plans."

"Which ones?" Jack asked.

"Every one of them. He'd happily blame me for tonight's storm if he could." Eve crossed her arms and gave a firm nod. "I will have words with him. If I'd been allowed to speak with

William Hunter at the town meeting, I could have been spared all this."

"How do you figure that?" Jack asked.

"Well, I would have made such a bad impression on him, William would have then gone out of his way to avoid me." Eve knew she would have been on her best behavior. However, that attitude didn't always serve her well. Whenever she tried to put her best foot forward, she somehow managed to get into trouble.

Jill cleared her throat. "I found an article about J.M. Kernel. There's talk about him being dropped by his publishing house and guess who owns it."

Finally, a solid reason to kill. "William Hunter," Eve said.

"Precisely." Jill drummed her fingers on the table.

"Maybe the author has something else lined up," Eve suggested, "If he's here, then we have to assume he's not holding grudges."

"Let's assume he is holding a grudge and let's also assume Stew Peters had a say in giving J.M. Kernel the boot. The author might have wanted to seek his revenge and somehow implicate William Hunter."

"So we're going to suspect the author because there's a rumor flying around," Jack said. "That should make my job easier."

Jill agreed with a nod. "We will suspect him until he can provide reasonable doubt."

They both gave Jack a sheepish smile.

"What do we know about Liz Logan?" Eve asked. "Remember, I didn't see her in the sunroom but then you said you served her a drink. I know I keep coming back to her, but I think she saw a window of opportunity and grabbed it."

"What madcap idea are you entertaining now, Eve?" Jack asked.

Eve pulled up a chair and sat next to him. "I'm only wondering where she could have been during that brief gap and I'm not having any trouble picturing her taking the box of cigars from her handbag and slipping out of the sunroom to put it on the dining room table without anyone seeing her. Until you can find out how those cigars got inside the inn, I'm happily going to suspect one of the guests."

"Okay, let's give the author a rest and focus on someone else." Jill got busy looking Liz Logan up online. "She's wife number two and has a keen interest in the arts. She sits in quite a few boards." Jill read out a list that included major art galleries and foundations. "She's been instrumental in getting William Hunter to donate part of his art collection. The negotiations are still ongoing."

Eve nibbled on a chocolate truffle. "There must be a motive in there somewhere. Keep digging. Maybe this is something else Stew Peters objected to." She shrugged. "Assuming he objected to anything."

"He came across as the type to veto his granny getting a life-saving operation. And I don't have to dig too deeply to find dirt on him. We know William is generous... when he wants to be. If Liz Logan wants to talk him into donating his art collection, only one man could stand in her way. Stew Peters. Bumping him off would clear the way for her."

"What sort of paintings are we talking about?" Eve asked.

"William owns a Picasso from the blue period. They're not my favorite. Too depressing," Jill said. "If I had the chance to acquire a Picasso, I'd select something more cheerful, like one of his Weeping Women."

Seeing Jack frowning, Eve explained, "Picasso used bolder colors and brushstrokes and most of the pictures are abstracts."

"Wow," Jill exclaimed. "I found an article about William's silver collection. Apparently, it's the finest in the world. It's housed in one of his properties in upstate New York. Can you imagine that? An entire house devoted to his collection."

"With any luck, he'll turn his leaky Rock-Maine Island house into a museum and only visit once a year." Eve finished her coffee and, glancing over at the sunroom, wondered if Mischief and Mr. Magoo would mind sharing the couch with her.

"Haven't you had enough for one day, Eve? Maybe you should think about getting some rest," Jack suggested.

"Eve and I can take turns curling up on the couch," Jill said. "We're not prepared to leave the kitchen unattended. I'll take the first shift. You need to be on your toes to catch the killer, Jack. So, you should go upstairs and have a good night's rest. Make sure to steer clear of the top floor rooms, just in case Martha Payne sprinkled ricin on the pillows."

Eve watched Jack's expression shift from amusement to resignation. By now, he knew it would be best to take the road of least resistance.

"There'll be an officer posted at the kitchen door throughout the night, so you can rest easy." He rose to his feet and hesitated. "If anything happens, holler."

"What if we're bound and gagged before we can call for

help?" Jill asked and gave Jack an apologetic smile. "Sorry, I'm stuck in worst case scenarios. They're streaming on a loop. And I'm usually the calm one."

Jack sunk back down on his chair.

Eve leaned her head on his shoulder. "You really don't have to stay here. Jill and I can look after ourselves."

"That's what I'm afraid of. I might have to rescue the killer."

Eve checked the clock. "I wish Mira would call to say she's arrived safely."

Jack frowned. "Did you ask her to call?"

"No, but after the scare I had when I thought she'd gone missing, she promised to never put me through that again."

"She'll be fine. Josh organized a police escort."

Hearing a knock on the door that led to the dining room, Eve shot to her feet.

Jill laughed. "That can't be the killer, Eve. They don't usually bother knocking."

Bracing herself, she opened the door.

"Hi. Sorry to bother you. I'm... I'm Miranda Leeds. I saw the light on and wondered if perhaps I might have some peppermint tea."

"Sure, I'll bring one out for you."

Miranda Leeds smiled. "Oh, wow. That's a stunning stove. Do you mind if I take a closer look?"

Surprised by the woman's interest, Eve said, "Feel free." In her experience, women who lunched rarely if ever stepped inside a kitchen or showed interest in what went on in there. Eve remembered seeing Miranda Leeds in the library when she'd come downstairs after her break. Engaging her brain, she also remembered there had been a man with her. Looking over Jill's shoulder, Eve read the list Jill had compiled and saw the name Marcus Leeds.

Her aunt had been in awe of William Hunter's ability to remain on good terms with his ex-wives. What did it say about the man when he also socialized with his ex's new husband?

"I'm in the process of remodeling my kitchen," Miranda explained. "As much as I love this stove, I doubt it would fit in there."

"There are smaller ones," Eve offered as she put the kettle on.

Miranda Leeds tucked her hair back and bent down to inspect the inside of the stove. It only then occurred to Eve she should be keeping a close eye on her.

"How is everyone holding up?" Eve asked. "Stew Peters' death must have come as a shock."

"Oh... We're all sort of drowning our sorrows."

"Did he have a pre-existing condition?"

"Not that we know of." Miranda continued to be more interested in the stove.

Eve didn't want to be overly critical. After all, everyone dealt with loss in their own way. "According to rumors, J.M. Kernel didn't get along with Stew Peters."

Miranda straightened and leaned against the kitchen counter. "I guess we all had issues with Stew, but that's to be expected when people spend a lot of time together."

"Did it ever get out of hand?" Eve asked.

Miranda chortled. "Stew went overboard once. Or rather, he was thrown overboard by Kernel."

"How did that happen?"

Miranda shrugged. "Stew was being his usual obnoxious self, critiquing Kernel's latest book. Actually tearing it apart."

Eve poured the tea and handed Miranda the mug.

"Thank you." She strode off only to stop. "I guess if I think about it, we all had reason to dislike Stew. Perhaps even enough to want him dead."

What a strange statement to make, Eve thought. "Really?"

"My divorce would have been more beneficial to me without him getting in the way," Miranda admitted, "Although, I really shouldn't complain. I married my divorce lawyer."

"And William doesn't mind socializing with him?"

"William's too easy-going to quibble."

Eve tilted her head. "I keep hearing good things about William. Why did you divorce?"

Miranda smiled. "He has a wandering eye and I prefer my men to be monogamous." She smiled. "That's probably his only fault." Shrugging, she thanked Eve for the tea and left.

Eve closed the door behind her. "Well, what do think about that?"

"I think they sent her in here to play mind games with us," Jill said. "She waited for you to ask her leading questions and didn't appear to mind answering them."

"Which means what?" Eve asked.

"That your reputation for catching killers has preceded you. That she wanted to give you some misleading information or she wanted to find out what we knew. I wouldn't believe anything she said."

"I found it interesting that she actually mentioned everyone having a reason to want Stew dead," Eve remarked. "Why bring up the subject of motive? As far as they know, Stew died from natural causes. No one mentioned murder."

Jill huffed out a breath. "I think we're going about this all wrong. We should be in there grilling them, one by one, until someone breaks. We could start with the author." Jill grinned. "He's a mountain of a man. It would be quite symbolic for him to crumble under our tenacious pressure. Then everyone else would follow."

Eve went to stand by the window and gazed out at the still stormy night sky. "It's strange. J.M. Kernel did not strike me as a violent man. In fact, he came across as a gentle giant."

Jill nodded. "I've formed the same impression so I'm going to put Miranda Leeds at the top of our person of interest list, right alongside her new husband, Marcus. Hypothetically, he might be the killer and she came in here to sow a few seeds of doubt and lead us on another trail."

"Is she covering for herself or her husband?" Eve asked.

"When she told you, she could have done better out of her divorce, I picked up on her resentment. Stew Peters had a hand in her not getting everything she wanted. That gives her motive." Jill sat up. "Actually, it's a perfect motive. She poisons a single cigar and sits back to wonder who will smoke it, her ex-husband or the accountant who deprived her of a bigger windfall. Either one would make her happy."

Jack sighed.

"Jack, you can sigh all you like. It's not going to stop Jill. And, for all you know, she might be onto something." Eve tried to settle down but she couldn't, so she strode around the kitchen and adjoining dining area. "When will the lab report come in?"

"Early morning," Jack said. "That should give you enough time to run through all the guests and point the finger of suspicion at them."

Eve smiled. "You're actually getting used to us brainstorming. You said that with a straight face." Hearing the kitchen phone ringing, Eve rushed to answer it. A quick glance at the caller ID told her it was her aunt. "Is everything all right, Mira?"

"Yes, dear. I just wanted to call and let you know we're home safe. It took us longer than expected because the police officer had to give the others an escort home. How is everything over at your end?"

Eve caught her up on the last half hour. "I'm worried about having left the kitchen unattended. Josh assures us no one came in but I'm on the brink of emptying the cupboards and throwing everything out."

"That's a bit extreme," Mira said, "Why don't you wait for the lab report to come in? For all you know, Stew Peters might have had a pre-existing condition."

"If that's the case, I wish he'd waited until tomorrow to die at William Hunter's place instead of at my inn. I don't care how inconsiderate that sounds. I'll never shake off this dark cloud. I swear, if one of the guests killed him, I will sue them for damages to my reputation." Eve crinkled her nose. "Hang on. I think I smell cigar smoke again." Eve set the phone down and turned to the others. "Can you smell that?"

Following the rich aroma, Jack and Eve rushed out of the kitchen.

They found William Hunter and J.M. Kernel outside on the front veranda smoking.

"Are you both out of your minds?" Eve made a grab for the author's cigar but, laughing, he skipped away from her. "You must have a death wish. Where did those cigars come from?"

William Hunter blew a smoke ring. Eve watched it hover for a second before a gust of wind swept it away.

Annoyingly, when Jack snatched the cigars from them, neither man put up a struggle.

Eve jabbed her finger against William Hunter's chest. "I'm going to sue you for... for emotional stress and... and defamation."

William Hunter threw his head back and laughed.

Eve made another grab for the man, but Jack restrained her by putting his arms around her waist and hauling her back.

William continued to laugh and then...

He bent over and coughed.

For a second, Eve thought he might have been chocking on his laughter, but then she saw his face turning blue. "He's chocking to death."

Chapter Nine

"QUICK, help him. He can't die here." Anywhere else but here, Eve thought.

Jack rushed to stand behind William and wrapped his arms around his waist. Grasping his fists, he pressed into William's upper abdomen with a quick upward thrust.

J.M. Kernel slumped down on a chair and gaped at them.

Jack continued applying the Heimlich maneuver. Finally, William dragged in a hard breath and whistled it out. Had he choked on his own saliva or had he inhaled something?

Eve pressed her hand to her mouth. At this rate, she might have to have the house vacuumed from top to bottom. Although, the idea of sterilizing it gave her more comfort.

William garbled something incoherent as he struggled to stand upright.

"I'll get some water," Eve offered. Turning, she found the other guests had piled up at the front door. She had to force her way past them to get inside. Jill had stayed behind in the kitchen. Thank goodness for Jill's common sense, Eve thought.

Filling a glass with water, Eve gave Jill a brief rundown of William's close call.

"Death by choking. On your veranda. He should have had the decency to wander away from your property."

"Just as well he didn't die," Eve said as she rushed off with the glass of water. A fourth death would have triggered another cycle of disasters.

William had managed to sit down. Eve heard the tail end of his assurance that he felt fine and there was no need to call the anyone.

"Oh, but you have to make sure you're all right," Eve said. "You need to spend at least a night in hospital. What if it happens again?"

Jack came to stand beside her and murmured, "Nice try, Eve. You're stuck with him. He's not budging."

"You could force his hand. You're an officer of the law," she whispered.

"He hasn't broken any laws, Eve."

"He's endangering himself and... Me."

"You? How so?"

"I'm thinking of my reputation. It's already fragile. Another death at my inn will incite a lynch mob. The entire town will rise up against me." Eve shivered. "Did you at least manage to find out about the cigars? I can't believe they would have smoked the same cigars that killed Stew Peters."

Someone behind her gasped and whispered to the person next to them.

A man approached them. Eve worked on a process of elimination and decided it had to be Marcus Leeds.

"Did we hear you correctly? Was Stew Peters killed?"

Eve shook her head. "The wind scrambled my words. Speaking of which, we should all go back inside. It's freezing out here."

No one moved.

"Fine. You can all stay out here and freeze." Eve stormed back inside. Striding into the kitchen, she asked, "Where were we?"

Jill looked up from the laptop. "You were talking to Mira and before that, we were pointing the finger of suspicion at Miranda Leeds."

Eve looked over at the phone.

"Don't worry, I told Mira you had to run off to deal with a situation."

"And what did she say?"

"She wasn't surprised and while she regretted leaving, on the way home she had a spark of an idea for her book so she was going to do some writing before going to bed. I believe tonight's events inspired her. Oh, and I told her to lock her bedroom door in case her editor turned out to be a serial killer. One never knows these days."

"I inspired her?" Eve asked, "Well, I'm always glad to be of help to Mira." Eve strode up to the back kitchen door and stopped, "I'm going up to get some blankets for us."

"Hang on, I'll come up with you."

With the police presence in the house, Eve now felt more confident leaving the kitchen unattended. Nevertheless, she went up the stairs two steps at a time and grabbed the first blankets she could find.

"What about pillows?" Jill asked.

Eve thought about it. "I really don't want to get too comfortable."

"Yes, but if you're going to get some shuteye, you should at least do it properly."

"Are you sure? These new pillows I purchased are magical. The moment your head hits the pillow, you fall asleep."

Jill laughed and then she stopped. "Oh, you're serious."

"Yes. I paid a king's ransom for them. They're hotel quality."

"I can't wait to move in... Assuming I'll be getting one of those pillows too." Jill looked over her shoulder. "I don't think anyone has come up yet."

"All right. We have pillows and blankets. You said you'd take the first shift, so I'm going to curl up and close my eyes for a bit." They made their way back down, both tuning in to the conversations wafting up from the living room.

"I just had a stray thought," Eve said as they hit the bottom landing. "Martha Payne's revolver. We should have put it away for safety."

Instead of answering, Jill nudged her and, pressing her finger to her lips, she signaled for silence and then pointed toward the kitchen.

Eve's eyes widened.

The refrigerator door stood open. Then they heard someone speak in a hushed whisper.

"I think I heard someone coming down the stairs."

Eve didn't recognize the voice. They had pillows and blankets as their only weapons. They'd have to do, Eve thought.

"I'm hurrying up," the person peering inside her refrigerator said.

Eve could only see part of her feet.

Mouthing a countdown even as Jill shook her head, objecting to whatever ludicrous idea Eve was proposing, Eve got to three and lunged forward. Jill, bless her soul, did not hesitate. She threw a blanket over the person at the refrigerator while Eve aimed for the other perpetrator using her pillows as shields.

The next few moments turned into a confusion of screams as they all struggled to either hold their captors or break free.

Eve thought she heard running footsteps approaching but then Jill yelled.

"You bit me."

A strong pair of arms wound around Eve.

"Let go, Eve. You'll smother the woman," Jack said.

"Only if you've got a hold of her," Eve growled.

"I've got her," he assured her.

Jill was still yelping from the bite she'd received. She'd let go of her prey only when Josh had rushed in to secure the woman in place, his arms clamping around the figure now covered in a blanket.

Jill held up her hand. "She left teeth marks."

Despite being restrained by two strong men, the intruders fought like wild cats.

"Get your hands off me, you brute," one said. "Police brutality."

"Only if you promise to calm down." Josh yelped. "Stop kicking."

It took some doing, but eventually, Jack managed to ask the woman he held to identify herself.

"I thought I had the right to remain silent," the woman exclaimed.

Josh didn't need to try so hard. Once the woman stopped wiggling around and promised not to kick him again, he pulled the blanket off her.

"Elsie?" both Jill and Eve exclaimed.

The leader of the Sisters in Crime reading group lifted her chin in defiance. "Yes. What of it?" Fixing her glasses back in place, she had another look around. "Oh, hello Eve. Jill."

"Elsie, what are you doing here?" Eve demanded.

"We got stranded in the rain." Elsie nudged her head toward the other person.

Eve had a proper look at the woman.

Jill elbowed her and murmured, "That's the town chronicler. I forget her name."

"Eleanor Parkinson," Eve said under her breath.

Jill chortled. "Looks like you have a rival troublemaker, Eve. Perhaps she'll take the load off you."

Eve sighed. "She can have my podium position, but she'll have to fight William Hunter for it. He's turned into quite a troublemaker. Hang on, is she a resident?"

"She's staying with me as my guest," Elsie McAllister said, her tone far too sweet considering the circumstances.

Jack cleared his throat. "Would either one of you like to explain what you're doing here?"

Eleanor Parkinson shook her head. "You don't have to say anything, Elsie. They haven't read you the Miranda."

Eve had caught a glimpse of Eleanor at the town meeting, but she hadn't had a proper look at her. At the time, she'd been fixated with William Hunter.

Dressed in a tweed ensemble, and wearing sensible lace up walking shoes, she had a friendly face with an easy smile. She reminded Eve of her school librarian, who'd always been eager to recommend books.

Jill elbowed Eve again. "She's really keen to give you a run for your money. I swear, if you'd been in her place you would have said exactly that."

"Officer, if you are arresting us then I believe we retain the right to remain silent and anything we say can and will be..." Eleanor Parkinson appeared to run out of steam, either that or she'd just realized she'd worked herself into a corner.

She was close to Elsie's age and the head of the Sisters in Crime Book Club didn't look a day over eighty.

"I feel dreadful," Eve said. "I could have hurt her."

Jill held up her hand. "I'm the youngest and yet I'm the only one injured. I think this will leave a scar."

Inspecting the bite mark, Eve had to agree...

"Elsie." Jack used his no-nonsense tone. "What have you got to say for yourself?"

Eve leaned in and murmured, "That hard tone never works on me. I doubt Elsie will cave."

Elsie appeared to rise in height. "As my friend said, either read us our rights or let us go free."

Sighing, Jack said, "No one is holding you against your will, but you need to explain what you were doing here."

Elsie's lip twitched. "We got stranded in the rain and took cover."

"Where?" Jack asked.

"You don't have to answer," Eleanor Parkinson said.

The town chronicler held on to her defiance. Eve couldn't help admiring her and wishing she would become a new island resident. She could really do with someone taking the spotlight away from her.

"Oh, it's all right, Eleanor. What is he going to do to us?" Elsie asked her co-conspirator, "We didn't do anything wrong."

Jack crossed his arms. "Unless you had permission to be here, you were trespassing, Elsie."

Eve rolled her eyes. "Jack. You're supposed to be encouraging her to talk. Instead you're trying to bully her into submission." Eve knew Elsie didn't have anything to do with Stew Peter's death, but she was up to no good.

Jack winked at her.

"I think Jack is humoring Elsie," Jill whispered.

Elsie lifted her chin. "I'll only talk if you offer me safe passage out of here."

Eve turned to Jill and asked, "Is Elsie trying to negotiate release terms with Jack?"

Jill nodded. "I'm waiting for her to ask for a helicopter out of the island."

Jack pulled out a chair. "Elsie. As I said, no one is holding you against your will. Please take a seat. You too, Eleanor. Would you like a glass of water or something to eat?"

Jill nudged Eve and whispered, "Jack's following the classic negotiation rules, steering the conversation to what he can provide and establishing goodwill."

Eleanor and Elsie looked at each other. Finally, they both gave a small nod. "We wouldn't mind something to eat. That's the reason we came into the kitchen. We thought everyone had gone to bed."

Jack looked over at Eve. She nodded and got busy preparing some sandwiches.

When she set down a couple of plates on the table, Elsie and Eleanor both inspected the contents.

"Would you like me to take a bite first?" Eve offered.

"That's all right," Elsie said, "I never took my eyes off you. Besides, I don't think I've given you any reason to poison me."

They dug in, eating the sandwiches with only the slightest hint of suspicion.

When they finished, Jack leaned forward. "Now, are you going to tell me what this is all about?"

Elsie sniffed. "I already told you. We took cover from the rain."

"Where?"

"In the stables." Elsie turned to Eve. "By the way, nice job converting the stables, Eve. I love the wallpaper."

Eve smiled. "Thank you." She knew she couldn't please everyone all the time, but it helped to hear someone appreciated her efforts.

"Why didn't you come in?" Jack asked. "Eve would have been only too happy to let you both take refuge in the house."

Elsie sat up. Eve suspected she was about to clam up again. Instead, Elsie shrugged. "We were on a reconnaissance mission."

Snooping around. She'd suspected as much earlier on when Elsie had appeared in the back veranda. Had Elsie acted of her own accord? "Who sent you?" Eve demanded.

Elsie shook her head. "We're not at liberty to say."

"I bet it was Roger McLain."

Elsie squared her shoulders. "If you must know, he's been beside himself with worry since hearing about William Hunter coming here for lunch. He wanted us to make sure nothing happened to him."

Eve threw her hands up in the air. "What did he think I'd do to William?"

Elsie exchanged a look with Eleanor. "We don't mean to cast aspersions on your character. However, you've been involved with a stabbing and a poisoning. Who knows what else you're capable of?"

Eve's eyes widened. "What? I was never charged or even held under suspicion."

Elsie gave a small nod. "You say that now. Those were lucky escapes."

"I had nothing to do with those deaths." Eve looked to Jack for support but he was busy shaking his head and brushing his hands across his face.

"You have a perfect set-up here and a perfect alibi. You've used your narrow escapes to build credibility," Elsie continued. "After all your close calls, the police won't hold you under suspicion. You might think you could actually get away with murder."

Eve could easily imagine Roger McLain asking Elsie to poke

her nose around the inn, but why would he encourage Eleanor Parkinson to come too? He'd asked the entire town to be on their best behavior. Surely he wouldn't want to convey the wrong impression.

"May I have some tea, please?" Elsie asked. She watched Eve preparing it; at one point even rising from her chair so she wouldn't miss any of the steps. "Have you made tea for anyone else today using tea from that tea caddy?"

Eve frowned. Why would she want to know that?

"I'm only being cautious," Elsie explained. "You might have a readymade mix of poisoned tea leaves."

If anyone had asked Eve to describe Elsie McAllister, she would have compared Elsie to the TV character Ms. Marple and mentioned her interest in mystery books. Their conversations, to date, had been brief. And at no point had Eve imagined Elsie having trouble distinguishing fact from fiction. Now... she wasn't so sure. "How about I drink some tea too?"

"I'm not silly enough to fall for that one. You probably have the antidote tucked away somewhere safe."

Sighing, Jack surged to his feet and strode out of the kitchen.

Eve guessed he needed to clear his head before Elsie forced him to renegotiate her terms of release. She considered going after him but then decided he probably needed some time to himself.

Jill laughed under her breath. "I think Elsie broke Jack."

"Strange. I just entertained the same thought." Eve rolled up her sleeves and gave Elsie a no-nonsense look. "Let's circle back to the reasons you came here."

Elsie looked over her shoulder. "Is Detective Jack Bradford coming back?"

"It's just you and me, Elsie."

Elsie looked at Jill. In response, Jill covered her eyes, her mouth and ears.

"All right," Elsie said as she made a show of shrinking back into her chair. "No need to get rough with me. I'll tell you everything. I wanted to give our town chronicler a scoop. I had the privilege of reading the first chapters and, let me tell you, it put me to sleep." Elsie turned to Eleanor Parkinson. "Sorry. Your writing is smooth but the subject matter let you down."

"A scoop?"

Elsie grinned. "Everyone knew you were going to slip up. Roger McLain should have known better than to issue a warning. Even without it, you're a marked woman and a magnet for trouble, Eve Lloyd. Ever since you returned from your cruise, we've been expecting something to happen, and you didn't disappoint us."

A magnet for trouble? Eve wanted to deny it. She should deny it. In fact, if she didn't, she'd only be encouraging people like Elsie McAllister to expect the worst from Eve. She'd never have any peace. Everyone coming to stay at her inn would become targets too.

"I knew if we hovered around long enough we'd witness something."

"And did you?" Eve asked. Elsie would have seen all the guests arriving and, if she'd taken her snooping seriously, she might have been peering inside windows and seen someone doing something incriminating.

Instead of answering, Elsie asked, "Does the police have any leads? Did one of the guests kill that man?"

"You have a vivid imagination, Elsie. No one killed anyone." Eve collected the plates and cups. As she cleared the table, she remembered Elsie and Eleanor had come snooping around at midday and it had started raining late in the afternoon. "Have you been hiding in the stables all this time?"

"Hiding? Us? Oh, no. I told you, we took refuge from the rain. We were... we were out walking. I wanted to show Eleanor around..."

"A moment ago you said you wanted to give her a scoop." Eve looked at the kitchen clock. At this rate, they'd never get to sleep. "You used the stables as your vantage point, admit it."

Elsie lifted her chin in a show of defiance. "I'll admit to no such thing. That would implicate me in nefarious activities. Eleanor and I were innocent bystanders caught up in your web of disasters."

Eve's mouth gaped open. One moment Elsie appeared to be encouraging Eve to provide the island with entertainment and the next, she was ready to join the mob to run her off the island.

"We didn't notice any of the guest leaving. Does that mean they're all under house arrest?" Elsie asked.

Both Jill and Eve rolled their eyes.

"This is your chance to give us your version of events, Eve. After tonight, we'll do as we see fit with the story," Elsie warned.

"What's that supposed to mean?"

"We'll be reporting the truth as we saw it."

"Exactly what did you see?" Eve demanded.

Elsie gave her a rundown of all the comings and goings they'd witnessed. It all seemed to match everything Eve knew.

Elsie pinned her down with her gaze. "Did you manage to put yourself in the clear again, Eve? You seem to have a knack for it."

"Only because I have no reason to be a suspect," Eve felt compelled to say. She knew Elsie wanted to bait her until she revealed something she could pass along to others or worse, until Eve incriminated herself. Anything she said, could and would be used against her.

"Everyone on the island knows you didn't like William Hunter because he's that type of man. After the town meeting, you returned home and plotted his downfall. Did you rope Mira into doing your bidding? I overheard her at the Chin Wag Café suggesting your inn would be a splendid place to host a luncheon. As far as anyone else knew, you had nothing to do with it. William Hunter came to you. You even went to the trouble of avoiding coming into town. So what went wrong?" Elsie leaned forward. "Did the wrong person drink from the poisoned glass?"

Eve hoped Jack had taken the whiskey glasses away for testing. What if Stew Peters had drunk poisoned whiskey? The moment Jack had mentioned the cigars Eve had run with the idea. Had that been Jack's way of diverting her attention?

Next time Mira complained about suffering from writer's block, Eve would suggest she talk with Elsie. She'd sort her out in no time.

Eve took the blankets and pillows to the sunroom but, seeing Mischief and Mr. Magoo stretched out on the couch and fast asleep, decided she and Jill would have to take turns in the easy chair.

"I suppose you came here on foot. I can't send you home now, so you'll have to make the best of it in the stables. You'll find blankets in the cupboard."

"You expect us to make our own beds?" Elsie asked. "For all we know, it could be our last night on this earth. We're taking quite a risk being anywhere near you. What sort of inn are you running here?"

Take it or leave it, Eve wanted to say but years of experience catering to customers won out.

As she strode out of the house, Elsie called out, "Don't forget the mint chocolate on the pillow."

Chapter Ten

EVE RETURNED from the stables and flopped down on the couch.

"Sorry I didn't go with you," Jill said, "I know I broke with protocol, but someone had to stay behind in the kitchen."

"That's fine, Jill. You had the officer standing outside the door and I had... Elsie. I doubt there is a killer within a thousand mile radius who would have risked coming anywhere near us. She is a force to be reckoned with. You wouldn't know it by looking at her. She looks so frail and delicate."

"My granny always says it's what lies beneath that counts."

Mischief and Mr. Magoo stirred.

"Sorry guys. I woke you up."

They looked at Eve with sleepy eyes, yawned and curled up again. A moment later, Mischief jumped off the couch.

"I knew that would happen," Jill said. "He needs a toilet break. If he doesn't wake up, he'll hold it right through the night.

Mr. Magoo is going to think about it for a bit," Jill clicked her fingers. "Come on. You know you want to go sniff around outside."

Mr. Magoo slanted his gaze toward Eve.

She grinned. "Yep, as soon as you jump off the couch, I'm claiming it for myself."

Jill rolled her eyes. "Why did you have to go say that for? You know he understands." Jill strode over and encouraged him. "Come on, you great big lump of fur. I'll turn the tap on and let it drip. You'll definitely want to go out then."

Jill's tough love worked a treat.

They both stood by the back door keeping an eye on the Labradors while they sniffed around and finally did their business.

Looking over her shoulder, Eve said, "Our guests have been very quiet."

Jill shook her head. "They haven't gone to bed yet. I wouldn't be surprised if we find them in the morning slumped on every available surface. Safety in numbers. It makes sense."

"Only if you have reason to worry," Eve mused. "Do you think they're onto the fact we're suspicious of them?"

"For all we know, they could be wondering if you had a hand in Stew Peters' death."

Eve bit the edge of her lip. She'd certainly given William Hunter reason to fear her. The way she'd poked him in the chest must have put him on notice.

Mischief ambled back inside the house while Mr. Magoo shot between Jill's legs and made a beeline for the couch.

"See, I told you he understands. He's calling dibs on the

couch. I think we'll both have to rough it on the floor. I don't suppose you have some sleeping bags stored somewhere?"

"Nope. Since I'm not the camping type, I've never had any need for them." Eve sighed. "I suppose I should put that on my shopping list. As much as I'd like to adhere to the belief this won't happen again, chances are... it will."

Using some of the chair cushions, she managed to fashion a mattress of sorts. "I'm setting my mental alarm clock to wake me up in a couple of hours."

Jill made herself comfortable at the table. "And I'm going to trawl around the Internet. Somewhere, there must be some information we can use to flush out the killer. I am determined to have a motive before Jack does."

"Usually, you have to find the culprit first." Eve didn't even bother plumping up the pillow. It felt heavenly. She pulled a blanket around her shoulders and, sighing with contentment, she closed her eyes and managed to fall asleep.

The sound of a hard demand woke her up. "Martha Payne's gun." Eve sprung upright. "Who said that?"

Jill laughed. "You did."

Eve rubbed her eyes. "How long did I sleep?"

"Two hours. Your mental clock beats anything made in Switzerland."

Eve scrambled out of the makeshift bed and straightened. "I have so many kinks to rub, I doubt I'll ever stand upright again."

She shuffled over to the dining room door and pressed her ear against it.

"You don't need to worry about them," Jill said, "They've all finally staggered to bed. One of the officers came in to let me know."

Eve edged the door open and glanced around the dark dining room. There were bound to be empty glasses to clear out, but she'd deal with them in the morning. However, she wouldn't mind having a look around. "Did I talk in my sleep?"

"No."

"My throat is dry and I have all this stuff swirling around my mind."

"Anything useful?" Jill asked.

"You should get some sleep first, I'll tell you later," Eve suggested.

"Are you kidding me?" Jill gestured with her hands. "Out with it, now before it fades away."

Eve sat down next to Jill at the table and rubbed away the remaining sleep from her eyes. "For starters, there was the gun."

"It should still be in Martha's coat."

Eve clicked her fingers. "I had a dream..."

"Yes, I know. You had everything worked out to perfection. You were going to open your inn; guests would arrive in droves, eat your wonderful food and go home happy. It will come true, some day."

Eve huffed out a breath. "In my dream, I saw someone wielding a gun. We were all herded toward the beach."

"And then?"

"I got into a pillow fight with Martha Payne. By the way, did you notice her shoes?"

"Were they in your dream?"

"Of course not. Why would I ask you about them if I'd dreamed them?" Eve pinched herself. "Am I still dreaming?" Glancing over at the kitchen clock, she groaned. Four in the morning...

"What about her shoes?"

"They're gorgeous. Embroidered satin in a rich navy blue."

"Interesting." Jill tapped her finger on her chin. "You woke up thinking about Martha's revolver and, out of nowhere, you mention her beautiful shoes. Your subconscious might be trying to tie her in to the murder."

Eve hauled herself out of the chair. "I'm hungry."

"It's the middle of the night, Eve."

"Tell that to my stomach." She made some toast. While she craved a strong cup of coffee, she opted for tea. At some point, she might want to take another catnap. If she didn't, there'd be hell to pay in the morning. "I haven't done this since I was a teenager. How long can you go without sleep?"

"No longer than eighteen hours," Jill said.

"But that's a normal day and now you've been without sleep for way longer than that. You must be exhausted."

Jill raked her fingers through her hair. "I think I'm running on adrenaline."

"Did you find anything online we can use to get the ball rolling?" Seeing Jill's puzzled look, Eve added, "To catch the killer."

"I believe I am now an expert on poisons. That could prove

problematic for me. If the police look into my online searching activities and ask me to explain my interest, I'll be in deep trouble."

"But you only started researching it tonight."

Jill bobbed her head from side to side. "That's not exactly true. Ever since the sushi murder, I've acquired a fascination for poisons. It comes and goes. Actually, I've been doing research every chance I get. I didn't mention it because you've been desperate to steer clear of trouble."

Eve set a pot of tea and a couple of mugs on the table and looked over Jill's shoulder as she scrolled through her search history.

"Can't you set it to automatically delete after a day?"

"You can, but the police have ways and means to track online activities."

Eve tapped her finger on the table. "Remind me—"

Jill put her hand up. "Give me a second. I created a document with questions to follow up on. Okay, shoot."

"Remind me to ask Jack if he's looking through everyone's online activities. If I had to buy a box of expensive cigars, I wouldn't know where to start looking. They're not available in every corner store. What am I saying? Of course, I'd start with an online search. Argh! I really need coffee."

She poured them both some tea and offered Jill some toast.

"No, thanks. I've been nibbling on chocolate all night."

Mischief wagged his tail in his sleep.

"He must be dreaming about chasing butterflies," Jill said.

When Eve finished her toast, she strode over to the adjoining dining room saying, "Let's snoop around. Someone might have dropped something or..." She shrugged. "Or left something behind." As she strode in, she turned lights on and collected empty glasses. Turning, she nearly dropped them.

Someone had stayed behind.

"Who's that?" Eve mouthed and pointed at the woman curled up on the couch.

"Julia Maeve. The newspaper editor," Jill whispered.

An empty bottle of whiskey sat on a table beside her. As Eve reached to remove it, Julia stirred.

"Where am I?" Julia plunged her fingers through her hair and moaned. "What time is it?"

"Four in the morning," Jill said. "Why didn't you go up with the others?"

Julia slumped back down and harrumphed. "My job is done," she slurred, "I'm not on the payroll 24/7."

Eve and Jill exchanged a puzzled look.

Julia appeared to have fallen asleep again. Nevertheless, Jill leaned down and murmured, "Was it your job to kill Stew Peters?"

Julia moaned.

"Was that a yes or a no?" Jill asked her, "Don't worry. You're off the record. You can tell me."

Eve tried to pull Jill up, but Jill wouldn't budge.

"Did William Hunter put you up to it?"

Julia Maeve murmured, "Keep 'em in line, he said."

"Who said?"

"All of them." Julia tried to roll over and nearly fell off the couch.

"Which is it?" Jill asked. "Did they all say it or did they all need to be kept in line?"

"I want a pony for Christmas." Julia flung her arm out and hit Jill smack in the face. "She always gets what she wants. Not fair. I want my pony."

Clutching her face, Jill rolled back, clearly biting her lip to stifle a moan.

Eve managed to drag her away. Once in the kitchen, she helped her back up to her feet. "Are you all right?"

Jill groaned. "I'm going to have a black eye. Ouch."

"Does it hurt?"

"Yes, and I just remembered Elsie bit me. So, it's a double ouch."

Eve rushed to the freezer and brought out a steak.

"Ouch. That's cold and hard. Is that a frozen steak?"

"Sorry. It's all I had. Hold it, I'll go see if I have something more suitable." Moments later, she returned with a bag of peas.

"Now my fingers are numb from the frozen steak," Jill complained. "I could get frostbite. My fingers could fall off. If they do, I'll have to learn to paint with my stubby fingers."

"How about some hot tea to calm you down? You're sounding jittery."

"I am calm," Jill yelped. Her teeth chattered. "And cold."

Eve put a blanket around Jill's shoulders.

"How's my eye looking?"

"Hard to say if it's red from holding the bags of frozen peas against it or the fistful of angst you got. Julia Maeve really wanted that pony."

"Yes, but did she have to take it out on me?"

Eve patted her on the shoulder. "You'll live."

"I hope I don't need a rabies shot."

Eve poured them both some more tea and mused, "Like you said earlier on, we've been going about this all wrong."

Jill grimaced. "Agreed. I should stop getting in the way of teeth and fists. At the rate I'm going, I wouldn't be surprised if I end up with a broken nose. But I guess that's not what you were referring to."

"I was thinking more about how little we know about them." Eve shrugged. "Yes, you've been researching them online, but that information only skims the surface. The guests are all well-to-do. We've been looking for motives in the obvious areas. Anything related to money."

Jill gave a small nod. "As the accountant, that made Stew Peters the money man."

"Yes, but there's more to it. He appeared to have played a pivotal role in the group, affecting everyone in William's inner circle, and not in a nice way. You described him as the proverbial detractor, finding fault with everything. Why did the Hunter group put up with him?"

"He wielded some sort of power over them, including William," Jill suggested and inspected the bite mark on her hand again. "Maybe he finally went too far and someone decided to take action. Or this could be a serial killer's first victim. We should wait until morning to do a head count. If there's another victim, then we'll have to rethink everything."

Eve nibbled the tip of her thumb. "Should we take Julia Maeve's sleep talk seriously?"

"Why not? It's a direct line to the inner workings of her mind."

"Yes, I can just picture us on the witness stand claiming we heard Julia confessing to killing Stew... in her sleep." Eve waved her hand. "Okay, I'm rambling. She said no such thing."

Jill smiled. "I think we can safely assume she alluded to it."

"Would you like to run that by Jack?"

"Oh, yes please. I'm waiting for him to develop a nervous twitch and that might just do the trick." After a moment's silence, Jill looked over her shoulder. "I wonder if they'll all make it through the night. Despite the interesting lead she gave us, Julia Maeve might actually be the most vulnerable one, curled up on the couch all alone."

My job is done...

What had Julia been referring to?

"I'll keep myself busy hunting down her by-lines," Eve said, "She might have written a disparaging article about someone. She's an editor, so I think we can assume her job involved... Let me think... spreading gossip?"

Jill cupped her chin. "We would have been scary during the Spanish Inquisition."

They sat in silence, listening to the wind whipping about then Eve said, "I'd like to know why William Hunter came to the island. He's a major player. This is an out of the way place. Too small and insignificant for the likes of him."

"You'd like him to be guilty of something."

Eve gave a small nod. "Yes." She had no trouble picturing him asking his assistant to find the perfect setting to stage a murder. Scooping in a big breath, she pushed it out and smiled.

"It would be a bonus. He might have had Stew Peters killed to cover something up. Some sort of dubious business activity comes to mind. But that wouldn't be specific enough for Jack to pursue."

"I wouldn't be so sure. Jack has a newfound appreciation of your instincts." Jill stretched. "I'm actually surprised we managed to get through most of the night without any serious mishaps."

"I wouldn't let my guard down just yet."

"It's always darkest before the dawn?" Jill asked.

Eve groaned. "What are the chances of this being death by natural causes?"

"I'll keep my fingers crossed for you, because I'm a good friend but I don't like our chances."

Eve looked out the window. "Elsie and Eleanor should be safe. When I left them, I heard them pushing the oak dresser against the door." Eve drummed her fingers on the table. "Elizabeth Rogue is a perfect candidate. No one mentioned her. Why is that?"

Jill said, "Because she's doing a great job of flying under the radar. I'll add her to the list. Jack is going to be a busy boy tomorrow... I mean, today."

"She's the one who organized the expensive water. I'm sure of it. She might also have been responsible for the cigars." What possible motive could she have? Disgruntled employee? A woman scorned? Working for William Hunter might have been her way of landing herself a wealthy husband and here he is, marrying his first wife again. Eve scratched her head. "Why do I keep thinking of William as the victim? He wasn't the target."

Jill looked up at the ceiling. "Oh, I remember. At one point, we thought Stew Peters was killed by mistake and William was the real target, but that's because you want him to be a target. Not because you're a bad person, but rather because his presence here has caused you grief."

"Thank you for clarifying that, Jill." Eve stifled a yawn. "You should try to get some sleep. There's no point in continuing our brainstorming session until the lab results come in."

Jill yawned. "You're assuming Jack will share the results with you."

"He knows there's no harm in me knowing."

"Only because you have ways of extracting the information out of him and, by now, he's learned to take the road of least resistance." Jill got to her feet and stretched. "Okay. I'm going to curl up and close my eyes."

Eve decided she wouldn't be able to sleep even if she tried.

The storm had moved on but, every now and then, she caught sight of a distant flash of lightning. She hoped it didn't rain again. That would mean another day of putting up with her unwanted guests.

As Jill settled down on the floor, Eve got busy doing some research reading the newspaper Julia worked for. Julia Maeve appeared to be strictly a behind the scenes editor. After a lengthy search, Eve failed to find a single editorial column written by her. She found a couple of reviews for J.M. Kernel's books full of praise for the author. Scanning through the last couple of issues, Eve twirled her fingers through her hair and battled through boredom and the temptation to research poisons. Jill had definitely appeared to enjoy herself discovering new ways to kill people.

She looked up some articles Jill had bookmarked and then pushed herself to read through another one of William Hunter's major newspapers.

"Oh, my favorite cookware is on sale. Fifty percent off," she whispered. Unable to resist, she went to the cookware's homepage and inspected each item on sale, earmarking the ones she would love to have. The next hour flew by as she read her horoscope, checked the weather forecast, and visited a rescue dog shelter.

"Jill is definitely better at researching." Disgruntled by her lack of progress, she set the laptop aside and remembered mentioning Martha's revolver but not doing anything about it. She should have suggested holding it in a safe place. Eve realized she didn't really have a safe place... or even a safe. "I should have a safe." Hotels had them. Did she wish to attract the type of guests who required safes? Not particularly, she thought.

She could include a condition in her bookings. "Leave the gun, bring the Cannoli." Grimacing, she wiped her mental slate clean. Some guests might miss the reference to The Godfather and think she was encouraging them to bring their own food.

Sunrise was still a couple of hours away. Her nocturnal ruminations would either yield a bounty of ideas and leads or it would drive her nuts. Eve bobbed her head from side to side. Either way, she'd be happy because, apparently, crazy people were not aware of their mental deficiencies.

Hearing a noise out in the hallway, she stilled. Her senses

didn't pick up on any other sounds. Rising to her feet, she tiptoed to the door and pressed her ear to it.

"Something's afoot," Eve murmured.

She heard muffled male voices.

Bracing herself, she edged the door open and peered out. A police officer stood talking with Josh who appeared to be clean-shaven and well rested. How had he managed that?

Seeing her, Josh nodded.

"Would you like some coffee?" she offered.

They both nodded, but neither one moved from their post.

"I'll bring it out." She prepared the coffee and a plate of cookies. "Anything to report?" she asked.

Josh shook his head. "With any luck, they'll be sleeping it off until midday."

Whose luck? Certainly not hers. She wanted them out of her inn as soon as possible. Reason told her there would be no avoiding having to prepare breakfast for them. Or brunch...

As Josh and the police officer sipped their coffees, Eve edged toward the cupboard where the coats were stored.

She had no idea what coat Martha Payne had worn. There were a couple of expensive looking women's coats, so she checked all the pockets. To her surprise, she came up empty.

No revolver.

Chapter Eleven

"I AM NOT PANICKING. I'm not." Eve wrung her hands and looked around the kitchen, searching for something to distract her.

Jill had stretched out on her makeshift bed, one arm resting on Mischief's shoulder. Eve didn't have the heart to wake her up and she really didn't see any reason to disturb her. Not yet.

Checking the time, she decided to get busy preparing breakfast.

As she set out a tray of bacon, Josh appeared.

"I've alerted Jack. He's on his way downstairs." He looked over at Jill and frowned. "Why is Jill's cheek red?"

"Oh, that... it's nothing. Last night she got in the way of Julia Maeve's fist. I'll make some coffee." The first slivers of daylight were making an appearance. The sky remained stormy but not threatening enough to stop William Hunter and his group from leaving.

"Could you run that by me again?" Josh asked taking a closer look at Jill's cheek. "When did it happen?"

Eve tried to recall the details. "I wanted to see if the guests had left any incriminating evidence behind and we found Julia curled up on the couch. Anyhow, Julia mumbled a few incoherent things in her sleep, which might be pertinent to the case. I know how that sounds, but I believe she would do just about anything to get a pony."

Josh opened his mouth to speak and closed it.

Eve huffed out a breath. "She has unresolved childhood issues."

"Does Jill think that too?"

Eve nodded. "Anyhow, Julia turned abruptly and her fist connected with Jill's eye. I guess it also caught her cheek."

Josh brushed his hand across his face and gave a small nod that appeared to be loaded with resignation. "How sure are you the revolver was in the coat?" Josh asked.

"When Martha Payne arrived, Jill took her coat and, when she put it away, she patted the pockets. That's how she found it."

"Did someone mention my name?" Jill moaned and, sitting up, she rubbed her eyes.

"Good morning," Eve said.

"Morning?" Jill looked toward the window. "It's still dark out there." When she looked at the kitchen clock, she yelped. "I have never been awake this early."

"Welcome to your first dawn," Eve said.

"It feels odd. It's as if I'm on a stage right before the curtain goes up."

Eve handed her a mug of coffee. "Drink up. You need this."

Jill waved at Josh who signaled to her eye.

"Oh, how does it look this morning?" Jill asked.

"A bit puffy... and red," Eve said. "You'll live."

Jill examined the bite marks on her hand. "So, what's been happening?"

Jack strode in and had a murmured conversation with Josh.

"I just heard my name mentioned again. What's going on?" Jill asked.

When Jack turned to answer, he noticed her eye. Luckily Josh filled him in. Somehow, he made it all sound perfectly normal.

"Will someone please give me a reason for being awake at this ridiculous hour?" Jill demanded.

Pouring herself a coffee, Eve said, "Brace yourself. Martha Payne's revolver is missing."

Jill drank her coffee in one gulp and jumped to her feet.

Eve turned to Jack. "Someone must have taken it late last night. What are you going to do about it?" In his place, she knew exactly what she'd do. All the guests would be dragged out of their beds and forced to stand out in the hallway while the police searched the rooms.

"As soon as the guests are ready to come down, we will ask for permission to search their rooms."

"Please, thank you and would you like a cherry on top?" Eve asked. "You can't be serious, Jack. You need to go straight up to Martha Payne's room. Right now. She has her revolver. I would stake my reputation on it."

"Your reputation?" Jack asked.

Jill went to stand beside Eve. They both lifted their chins. "Yes," they said.

Jack drew in a deep breath and gave the platter of bacon a longing look.

"You can forget about breakfast," Eve warned.

"Oh, that's harsh," Jill remarked. "Do you really want him to storm into Martha's room on an empty stomach?"

"No one is storming anywhere," Jack said. "There's an officer standing guard outside her room. She's not going anywhere."

"Fine, I'll take pity on you and make you a bacon sandwich, but I feel I should say you are lacking a sense of urgency."

"You'd like me to go into a state of frenzy?" Jack asked.

"What could be worse than knowing there is someone in this house wielding a weapon?" A weapon they most likely wished to have nearby for self-protection, Eve reasoned. She knew she shouldn't jump to conclusions. Martha probably had a good reason to carry a gun.

An officer stepped up to the door. When Jack strode up to him, they spoke in hushed whispers. Eve did her best to try to overhear what they said, but they'd both turned their backs on her.

Mischief and Mr. Magoo stirred awake and ambled over to Jill.

"Nature calls," Jill said.

"I'll come with you. Let's go out the front. I need to grab a couple of jackets."

The moment Eve opened the front door, Jill shivered. "Owning cats would make my life so much easier. I'd only need to set up the litter box and forget about them."

They both scooped in big breaths and stepped out onto the

veranda.

Mischief and Mr. Magoo raced down to the front yard and made quick work of finding their favorite spots.

Eve wondered what her neighbors would say about having their quiet lives disrupted by yet another death brought to them courtesy of Eve Lloyd, the local mad innkeeper.

"What are you chortling about?" Jill asked.

Eve looked over her shoulder. "I'm actually wondering if I should have brought a rolling pin with me. We're defenseless out here."

"Don't worry, I've got your back."

They'd already faced a rifle wielding mad woman and they'd also had a revolver pointed at them. Pointed and fired, Eve mentally added. "I think I have become impervious to danger. A part of me says I should take care and be on guard, but experience has taught me no amount of preparation can ever be enough."

Jill jumped on the spot. "What would you call this weather?"

"Brisk." Eve cupped her hands and blew into them. "They've done their business, what are they doing now?"

"Sniffing around," Jill said, "I call it the doggy grapevine. This is how they keep up with what's going on in their world."

Eve noticed Mischief slanting his gaze toward her. "I think Mischief just read a doggy message that probably alerted him to the local mad innkeeper." She looked at the line of cars parked along the street. Narrowing her gaze, she frowned. "That's odd." She pointed at a white SUV. "It's all fogged up. Do you think someone is making out?"

Jill took a step only to be hauled back by Eve.

"Where are you going?" Eve asked in a hard whisper.

"To investigate, of course. Don't you want to know who's inside the car? It could be someone taking their last breath."

"I don't know," Eve said, "There's being nonchalant about not carrying a weapon to safeguard us against a possible surprise attack and then, there's willful disregard for our safety. Also, last night is still fresh in my mind. I feel dreadful about tackling Elsie. Could we, for once, be sensible and call Jack?"

"Where's the fun in that?" Jill laughed. "Besides, I really don't care to be mocked and he's been having quite a few laughs at our expense."

Eve turned toward the house. She'd give anything to lead an ordinary life. "It's too late now."

"What are you mumbling about?" Jill grabbed hold of her arm and tugged her along.

"I'm entertaining a few wistful thoughts about what might have been and what obviously can't be because I'm on some sort of treadmill and I can't jump off it."

They approached the SUV from the back. Belatedly, Eve realized that would give the occupant an advantage, as they would no doubt be able to see them on the side mirrors. Signaling to Jill, they both crouched down and split up.

"This is no longer a bad idea," Eve said under her breath, "It's dreadful." Worse case scenarios flooded her mind. The occupant swinging the door open and slamming it against Jill's nose. The occupant firing at them. "Oh, help." Until now, she'd assumed someone inside the house had helped themselves to a handy weapon.

Eve shook her head. Jill had asked for this and she'd already had two close calls, which had served as warnings, so she couldn't complain. Nevertheless, Eve got down on all fours and looked under the vehicle. Jill was on the other side and almost parallel with Eve. She picked up a pebble and threw it at her. It bounced off Jill's ankle.

Jill hit the ground and glared at Eve, mouthing, "What?"

Eve curled her fingers and fashioned a revolver out of her hand. Instead of being alarmed, Jill appeared to become more determined. Fine, Eve thought. With any luck, she'd be able to someday tell her grandchildren about her adventures.

Their hand gesture communication continued with Jill holding up three fingers. "Okay," Eve mouthed as she assumed Jill wanted her to count to three. A few more hand gestures later, Eve also assumed they had reached some sort of consensus and now needed to put a plan into action. Then again, Eve had never been any good at charades.

She eased her way toward the driver's door, counted to three and, springing to her feet, wrenched the door open at the same time Jill opened the passenger door.

When the occupant screamed, both Jill and Eve jumped back. Later, Eve would think their minds had acted on a time delay, registering the image of the occupant swinging a revolver from one to the other. They both teetered and threw themselves to the ground, rolling away and crashing into each other under the SUV.

"It's a woman," Eve murmured.

Hearing her scrambling to climb out of the SUV, they threw themselves into action, this time, presenting a united, take-no-prisoners front.

For once, luck worked in their favor and they caught the assailant from behind.

Jill clamped her arms around the woman's neck and pulled her back, her deep growl catching Eve by surprise. Although, it didn't impede her reflexes as she reacted by snatching the revolver from the woman's hands. Or, at least, trying to.

A cacophony of confusing growls, screeches, yelps and grunts mingled with the sound of their shoes scraping on the ground and Mischief and Mr. Magoo's barking.

When the woman went limp, Eve screamed, "Don't fall for it, Jill. Hold tighter."

"I will. You focus on grabbing the gun," Jill yelled back.

Easier said than done, Eve thought.

She lifted her gaze and met the woman's eyes.

Julia Maeve. The newspaper editor.

"Let go," Eve growled and put all her might into taking possession of the weapon. "I'll bite you."

Julia Maeve's eyes widened.

"She will," Jill said. She somehow managed to twist her arm around and extended her hand to show Julia the bite marks on her hand. "See. I've got the bite marks to prove it."

Julia Maeve conceded defeat by once again going limp. This time, she released her hold on the gun. Of course, she didn't make an announcement so Eve stumbled back and fell on her butt.

"You're both mad," Julia spat out.

"Yeah? What were you doing in your car armed with a revolver?" Eve demanded.

"Trying to stay alive. Do you think I wanted to spend the night under the same roof as a killer?"

Eve lifted her chin. "It's all conjecture and far too premature to think someone killed Stew Peters."

Julia Maeve harrumphed.

Eve jabbed a finger at her. "You know something."

Julia pulled her gaze away, tugged her jacket and strode off toward the house saying, "Shouldn't you be busy preparing breakfast?"

Jill nudged her, "Well? You can't let her get away with that. Go on, say something back."

Eve narrowed her gaze. "There's something going on here."

"Really? You don't say?"

Eve bent down to give Mischief and Mr. Magoo a scratch. "You guys did great." She looked up and saw Jack and Josh standing on the veranda. Eve waved the revolver. "We're fine. Thank you for asking." As she returned her attention to the Labradors, she caught sight of Elsie and Eleanor peering at them from the stables.

Eve groaned. "Just great. Our altercation was witnessed by Elsie and the town chronicler. What are the chances they won't embellish their version with a few gunshots?"

"Next to none," Jill said.

Elizabeth Rogue stood at the kitchen door placing the orders for breakfast. "William prefers his toast crispy. Can you manage that?"

Eve counted to ten and when she still sensed a barrage of words begging to be released, she counted to ten again. Playing it safe, she nodded. Who knew what would come out of her mouth if she opened it.

"Please take his breakfast up at precisely nine o'clock. He enjoys his coffee piping hot."

Eve stretched her lips into a wide smile and again nodded. Jill saved the day by stepping up and taking the piece of paper from Elizabeth Rogue and saying, "No one makes piping hot coffee. It tastes foul and the Sea Breeze Inn has a reputation to uphold. We'll happily supply him with a pot of boiling water on the side." As she spoke, Jill seemed to rise in height.

"I suppose he'll have to settle for that." Elizabeth swung on her Gucci loafers and left.

Jill performed a dance on the spot. "Sorry, I couldn't help myself. I guess I'm now out of a job."

"On the contrary," Eve smiled. "We need someone who can think on their feet."

"In other words, every inn should have a snarky chambermaid. I'll try to remember to shuffle my feet when I take his lordship's breakfast in."

"Elizabeth looked well rested," Eve remarked. "And well dressed. How did she manage that?"

"I saw her go out to her car and retrieve a carry bag. I guess she's the type who's always ready for any occasion."

Jack rose from the table and took his empty mug to the kitchen. "Thank you for breakfast, Eve."

"And for saving you the trouble of frisking the guests," Jill said. "Think of the time we saved you by tackling Julia Maeve."

"You're lucky she's not pressing charges."

"She wouldn't dare," Jill said. "She stole that revolver. We're the ones who should be making a fuss."

When Jack's cell rang, he excused himself and went out the back door.

"Fingers crossed that's the lab results coming in. The sooner he can haul someone off to jail the better." Eve arranged the first breakfast tray. Miranda Leeds and her husband had ordered fruit, cereal and juice, but strangely, no coffee. All the guests appeared to be in their late forties and they mostly looked to be in good shape. With one exception, Eve thought. The author showed signs of leading an indulgent lifestyle and if Jill hadn't told her he'd just hit forty-nine, Eve would have thought he'd be in his late fifties.

"Is this one ready to go?" Jill asked.

"Yes."

"You're deep in thought."

"I'm thinking how odd William Hunter is. Most men in his place would look for a trophy wife, someone much younger. Instead, he's always married women around his age."

"Don't you just hate him? He's turning out to be a regular nice guy."

Eve shrugged. "My contact with him has been limited to me jabbing a finger against his chest. I still find him... obnoxious."

Josh appeared at the kitchen door. "Ready?"

"Ah, my escort has arrived." Jill grinned and picked up the breakfast tray. "Lead the way."

Eve watched them leave and nodded at the officer who came

to stand by the door. They were not letting their guards down, not for a minute.

By the time Jill returned, Eve had two more breakfast trays ready for her.

"Yum. Cinnamon toast. I think I'll be ready for a second breakfast soon."

"Did they give you any trouble?" Eve asked.

"Would you believe it? Miranda and Marcus were both doing yoga. They must have had their gear in their car too."

"Didn't Marcus Leeds spend the night drinking?"

Jill nodded. "He must have a strong constitution."

"You should get going. I'm about to start his lordship's breakfast." Eve wiped a plate clean and checked it again for smudges. Luckily, she'd stocked up on basic ingredients so had no trouble putting together the full breakfast of eggs, bacon, sausages, mushrooms and tomatoes. Belatedly, she realized she'd been left alone in the kitchen. "I could poison him and no one would know."

When Jill returned, she put the kettle on.

Eve laughed. "You weren't kidding about the boiling water."

"I know how you feel about your coffee and I listened to your instructions." Jill tapped Eve's new toy, an Italian coffee machine with all the bells and whistles. "The perfect brewing temperature is very important. It should be between 195F and 205F. The closer to 205F the better. Boiling water should never be used, as it will burn the coffee. If he wants to ruin it, he can do it himself." Jill searched the cupboard for a small jug. "In fact, I'm surprised you're not putting your foot down."

"Would you like me to storm into his room and set him

straight?"

Jill giggled. "I love it when you pander to my quirks." She inspected the trays. "I wonder how Valentine manages with her cup of green tea and five almonds. She's slim, but she's also very tall. Where does she get her energy from?"

"William must prop her up," Eve suggested. "When you come back, we can sit down to a proper breakfast."

Jill turned only to stop. "Out of curiosity, do you think any of your future guests will want breakfast at the crack of dawn?"

"If they do, they can stay elsewhere. Breakfast will be strictly served from eight in the morning onward."

Jill nodded, "I'll make sure to include it on the webpage."

Eve gazed out at the gray sky and wondered if she'd need to include full disclosure on the website. "Interesting facts about the Sea Breeze Inn... There have been three deaths but the owner has a knack for..." Eve tapped her chin, "Stumbling upon killers?"

Jack strode in, his face set in such a way that Eve knew she'd have to extort whatever information he was intent on withholding.

"Talking to yourself, Eve?"

"Jack, please tell me we survived the night because we had no reason to worry... because Stew Peters died of natural causes."

"Sorry, I can't lie to you."

"And?"

"It's official. This is now a murder investigation."

Jill took a long sip of her coffee and looked up. "I think this is the first time we've sat in silence for longer than five minutes."

Eve remained speechless. Entertaining ideas of a murderer on the loose had, in a roundabout way, been their way of coping with the situation, but that had been last night. This morning they had to deal with the reality of it all.

"Did Jack say anything about a plan of action? He can't possibly think they can all stay here another night." Jill brushed her hand along her cheek. "I'm a strong believer that what doesn't kill me, makes me stronger, but I'm not sure I'm prepared to suffer any more injuries. So much for Jack warning us to travel in pairs. In both instances, I was with you."

Jack had a lot to answer for. He'd deliberately avoided answering any direct questions. When he returned from making his rounds, Eve shot to her feet and demanded, "Did I poison Stew Peters?"

"Is that what you've been worrying about all this time?" Jill asked. She turned and glared at Jack. "How could you leave her guessing?"

Jack's eyes widened slightly. "I came in here for coffee."

"You want coffee? You'll have to go through the third degree first." Jill stood toe to toe with Jack. "In hindsight, I wish I hadn't stood up for you and insisted Eve should make you breakfast. Rest assured, it will not happen again. You're on your own, buddy."

The edge of Jack's lip lifted. Sighing, he said, "Jill's right. You have a right to know, but can you promise me you won't use the information to confront any of the Hunter crowd?"

The obvious answer nearly tripped out of Eve. Of course, she'd do and say anything to get some details.

Just say yes, Eve.

"Eve!" Jill exclaimed. "Go on. Say yes."

She tried to say yes again, but the word simply wouldn't budge. Eve gave Jill an exasperated look and threw her hands up in the air. "What good is having exclusive information if you can't use it?"

"That's what I thought," Jack murmured.

"Fine. I promise, but only if you promise to get them all out of here. Today."

"For starters," Jack said, "There was only one cigar missing from the box."

"What?" Jill pointed a finger at Jack. "You've known that all along and didn't say anything."

Eve sat back. "Hang on. How can that be? Both J.M. Kernel and William Hunter were smoking."

Jack leaned against the kitchen counter. "Yes. William always carries two cigars with him. He doesn't like smoking alone and the author has always been his smoking buddy. His personal assistant, Elizabeth, keeps a stash of cigars for him."

Eve played around with the information. This had to be common knowledge among the Hunter set.

Jack continued, "Stew Peters had quit smoking years ago."

Eve groaned. "Don't tell me he suddenly had the urge to take it up again."

"According to William Hunter, Stew asked for a cigar. William and the author had already started puffing on their cigars, so William came into the house to fetch the box he'd remembered seeing."

"That means the killer didn't target Stew Peters deliberately."

Eve shot to her feet. "Or... either the author or William Hunter egged him on knowing he'd have to have a cigar from the box..."

Jill strode around the kitchen and stopped. "Jack, you've left something out. Are you ready to admit at least one of the cigars had some sort of poisonous substance?"

He nodded.

Jill put a hand up. "Wait. If it was only one cigar, then the killer really intended playing Russian roulette. He didn't care which one smoked it. But if all the cigars were poisoned, then he wanted to kill more than one person. Or rather, he wanted to kill all the cigar smokers in the group." Jill turned to face Eve.

"The killer is a woman," they both said.

"You're forgetting someone," Jack said.

Eve clicked her fingers. "Miranda Leeds' husband."

Jill agreed. "He was the only man who didn't go outside to smoke."

Jack's phone rang. Before he could take the call, Eve grabbed his hand. "Don't you dare leave without telling us if all the cigars were poisoned or not."

Jack nodded. "The entire box was contaminated."

Jill growled. "He could have started with that. Instead, he watched us running around in circles."

Eve smiled. "Knowledge is power and I think Jack has learned to add more value to it by wringing out as much enjoyment as he can."

"At our expense."

The entire box of cigars. Poisoned. Either the killer wanted to kill all the cigars smokers or they were sure only Stew Peters would have a cigar from the box.

Chapter Twelve

"WILLIAM HUNTER IS LEAVING," Jill announced.

Eve wiped her hands dry. "Please tell me he's taking everyone with him."

"Sorry," Jill shrugged. "He's going up to the house to check on the water damage. I heard him say he wanted to make sure there are enough rooms to accommodate his guests. And if there aren't... You could impose a levy fee for duress."

"The house is huge. How could he not have enough rooms?" It sounded like a likely story to Eve who hadn't completely discounted the theory of William setting her up and using her inn as the ideal scene for his crime. What if he wanted to kill someone else? "The storm's moved on. If he can't accommodate them, they should all go home. Party's over, people."

"What if Jack told them they can't leave the island?" Jill walked around the kitchen table straightening chairs. "I picked up a strange vibe from the others. There are a couple sitting out on the veranda. Miranda and her husband are in the library. They seem to like it there. You'd think they'd all be sitting together. I can't shake off the feeling they'd rather steer clear of each other."

"I told you there's something going on. Julia Maeve knows something and what she knows is bad enough for her to steal a revolver and seek refuge in her car."

"You might be right," Jill said. "When Miranda Leeds came in to ask for a cup of tea last night, she more or less admitted they'd all had reasons to want Stew Peters dead."

These people had known each other for a long time, Eve mused. What kept them together? Why had the author tolerated Stew Peters' condescension? Could they be harboring secrets?

"You look puzzled," Jill said.

"That's because I am."

"Heads up. Elsie and Eleanor are coming. I suppose they want breakfast."

"Is it safe to come in?" Elsie asked. Seeing Jill's red cheek, Elsie gasped.

Eve waved them both in. To her surprise, they sat at the table but didn't say anything. Offering them a bright smile, Eve asked, "What would you ladies like for breakfast?"

Still looking at Jill's cheek, Elsie said, "If it's not too much trouble, tea and toast, please. We're both partial to English marmalade."

They both clasped their hands and sat perfectly upright.

"I trust you slept well," Eve said.

They offered her a small nod.

Jill strode up to the table and set a bowl of sugar down, all the while giving them a lifted eyebrow look. "You're not very chatty this morning."

"We don't want to cause any trouble," Elsie said. "We only need some sustenance to get us going and then we'll be on our way."

"You came here on foot. Surely you're not planning on walking back." Jill looked over at Eve and winked. "Perhaps I could give you a lift back to town."

"I... we wouldn't want to inconvenience you."

"Oh, but it would be a perfect opportunity to get our stories straight." Jill gave the town chronicler a pointed look. "Have you thought about what you'll write?"

"Yes," Elsie said, "We've agreed to keep quiet about everything we saw here yesterday and early this morning." Elsie leaned forward and looked at Eve. "We promise we won't say anything."

Jill set the cutlery down. "If you talk, we'll know about it. We have ways of finding out."

They both crossed their hearts and ate their breakfasts in silence. When they finished, Jill told them they could wait in the library and she would give them a lift back in a while.

"I think that went rather well," Jill said.

Eve wagged a finger at her. "You should be ashamed of yourself. You've made an elderly woman afraid of you."

Jill held up her hand. "She bit me. I'm going to bear this scar for the rest of my life."

Eve looked out the window and gestured to Jill. "Julia Maeve and Liz Logan are on the beach talking." The newspaper editor and William's ex-wife were deep in conversation, and Eve would bet anything they were not discussing what they would wear to Stew Peters' funeral.

"They're arguing," Jill said.

"How can you tell?"

"Julia's hands are curled up into tight fists."

Eve eased the window open and strained to hear them but the squawking seagulls made it impossible.

"I need to learn to read lips," Jill mused. "That would be a handy skill to have. If I had to guess, I'd say Julia is telling Liz it's no longer safe to be around William Hunter. I'm going to go out on a limb and also say she's trying to form an alliance with Liz. If they joined forces, they could go up against him."

Eve tilted her head. "Because he'd holding something against them?"

Jill grinned. "A secret. With Stew Peters gone, William has lost his leverage and they now see their chance to break away."

"I want to like your theory," Eve said, "But that would expunge William of any wrong doing. If Stew Peters was the reason they all stuck together, William would not want him dead."

Looking over her shoulder, Jill whispered, "Don't worry, Eve. I'm sure we'll be able to pin something on him. With Stew gone, William might be driven to do something desperate. Maybe he's gone up to his house to set a plan into motion. That reminds me, Jack said the whole box of cigars was contaminated but he didn't mention anything about the poison used."

"Have you ever known Jack to willingly divulge information?" Eve stacked the breakfast dishes in the dishwasher and glanced around the kitchen looking for any stray mugs. "We're sleep deprived and not functioning at our best."

"Looks like we arrived just in time," Mira said as she strode into the kitchen.

"Mira!" Eve threw her arms around her.

"I'm so glad you made it through the night. I brought Jordan for breakfast. I'm afraid you've spoiled me, Eve. I've become so accustomed to you cooking for me, I can't even find the coffee canister."

"Breakfast coming right up," Eve said.

"Any news?" Mira's editor asked.

Eve tried to remember if Jordan Monroe had fallen under suspicion. Yes, he had, mostly because he'd had some handy information. "Jill will fill you in. I'm afraid I'm sleep deprived so anything I say will sound jumbled." Eve set to work preparing a full breakfast. For the first time that morning she threw herself into the pleasure of cooking.

"Have you come up with any new theories?" Mira asked.

Jill pointed at the two women out on the beach. "They're conspiring. We're sure of it." Jill then proceeded to tell them about Julia Maeve's nocturnal blabbering and taking refuge in her car. "She must have known about Martha Payne always carrying a revolver. Or maybe, when she decided to go out to the car, she went to get her coat and that's when she found it. Eve's convinced she knows something significant but is too afraid to talk about it."

Mira smiled. "You might be onto something. I have a gift for you." Mira held up a magazine.

Wiping her hands dry, Eve took the magazine. "This is twenty years old."

Mira nodded. "Last night I came across a few references online to articles about William Hunter and one of them stuck in my mind. The article predates the Internet so I doubt it's online, but then I remembered the stacks of magazines I'd found at the bookstore. I had one box in the house, but the rest are still in storage."

"The ones you said you'd go through on a rainy day when you had nothing better to do?" Eve asked.

"Yes. Those ones. Anyway, last night I tossed and turned so I decided to have a look. I found an article about William Hunter's silver collection and another one about his house in Rhode Island. At first, I thought the article was about the life of the rich and famous because it went on and on about the house's history. One of his ancestors built it during the Gilded Age. It's near The Breakers."

"That sounds familiar," Eve said.

"It's a massive house built by the Vanderbilt family in Newport, Rhode Island. Cornelius Vanderbilt commissioned it in 1893. I had a wander around it last year and found it inspiring for one of my books."

"Fancy living in a seventy room Italian Renaissance style palazzo," Jill said as she read from the Internet. Her mouth gaped open. "I'd settle for the stables. My goodness. Listen to this. The stables were 100 feet deep and 150 feet wide. The lady of the house would send a day-book every morning with a list of the carriages that would be used that day. When a carriage was requested, the horses were brought out, hitched and left the building from the north door. All the returning carriages entered through the south door. The twelve grooms and stable boys employed lived directly overhead and they had access to a large kitchen, dining room and living room."

Mira patted her hand. "You have your own stables, Jill."

Jill sat up and shifted in her chair. "Yes, I do, and I wouldn't mind sharing it with a couple of horses."

"Sorry, Jill. I'm going to have to nip that idea in the bud." Seeing Jill's disappointment, Eve shook her head. "At least for the time being." She returned her attention to the magazine and pointed at a photo. "Is that the William Hunter group?"

"Yes, and this is the Hunter cottage."

A cottage? The house looked massive.

"But this is what I wanted to show you," Mira pointed to a group photo. "They've been getting together for years, going back to their youth. This photo was taken at William's twenty-first birthday bash. It was a weeklong affair with a who's who guest list."

Eve shook her head. "This annoys me. Why come to my inn when they have such a splendid playground at their disposal?"

"He likes to travel around and rarely spends more than a couple of weeks in one place."

The first thought that popped into Eve's mind had her smiling, "What is he running away from?"

They all looked at her.

"That is a very good question," Jill said. "It fits in with your theory."

"You have a theory?" Mira asked.

"Yes. We've been playing around with the idea they all have

something to hide. It's something that keeps them glued together, whether they like it or not. What if..." Eve clicked her fingers. "Oh, what if something happened way back then and one of them witnessed it and used the information to control the group."

"That person being Stew Peters?" Mira asked.

"Yes. He fits the profile of someone devious enough to use anything to wield power," Eve said.

"A profile?" Mira asked.

Eve shrugged. "A character trait. Jill called him a proverbial detractor. We've decided he knew something and it gave him leverage over the others."

Mira exchanged a look with her editor and tapped the magazine. "Perhaps you should look at this photo and compare it to this other one. Let's see if you notice something different."

"Picture games. I love those." Jill strode up and looked over Eve's shoulder.

"Yes, and since you're the artist, you'll be able to spot the difference in no time." Eve's gaze jumped from one image to the other. "It says here the photos were taken during that birthday week."

They both moved closer to the window to take advantage of the natural light.

Eve guessed the photos had been taken a day apart. "Okay, they look happy in the first picture, and somewhat strained in the next one. They're still smiling, but the smiles look forced." Had something happened between the time the photos were taken? They were all attending a birthday celebration. She could see bottles of champagne on a table. Quite a few of them... "They look apprehensive." She'd bet anything the moment the photographer put his camera down they all looked over their shoulders.

Jill pointed at one of the photos. "I think that's Julia Maeve and she's the only one looking away. Also, so far, she's the only one who's crumbled slightly at the edges."

"Last night you said she looked as if she was observing everyone."

Jill nodded. "Yes, taking note of everything. Then again, she's a newspaper editor. It would be an ingrained trait."

"Authors are observant too," Eve said, "Yet J.M. Kernel seemed to be rising above everything. Aren't authors supposed to be glum?"

Mira lifted her chin. "Am I ever glum?"

Eve laughed. "Not even when your mad innkeeper is giving you trouble." Sighing, she gave it some more thought. "Okay. The author is the type to adapt to changing circumstances. He's good at pretending everything is okay." Eve tapped the magazine. "Something happened all those years ago, and now... it's come back to haunt them."

"I know what you did last summer." When Mira looked puzzled, Jill explained, "It's a film about these friends who are stalked by a killer a year after they covered up a car accident they were all involved in."

Eve grabbed Jill by the shoulders. "Yes!" she exclaimed, "For some reason, my mind was only skimming the surface and thinking someone might have had an affair or walked in on someone and seen something they shouldn't have. They are all guarding a dark secret. I didn't even meet Stew Peters, but from what I've heard, I would not have given him the time of day.

Someone did something dreadful, he witnessed it and he was the type to use the information to his advantage."

"Or," Jill grinned. "William witnessed something and he then confided in Stew Peters." Jill strode around the kitchen. "Think about it. He's not likable. We know he doesn't have any family. A person like that is bound to end up alone, cast adrift. Ostracized. He won't change his character. In fact, he thrives on being a detractor and he's found a way to remain true to himself and get away with it."

"Yes," Eve exclaimed and pumped her fist in the air.

Mira and her editor exchanged raised eyebrow looks.

"You were right, Mira. They are good," Jordan Monroe said.

"Yes, I only wish they would now pass the information onto the authorities and let them take care of it." Mira sighed. "Knowing Eve, she'll promise to do just that and be side-tracked along the way, meaning, she'll end up having a gun pointed at her." Mira wagged a finger at her. "Don't think I didn't notice the fresh coat of paint on my wall, Eve."

Eve gave her aunt a sheepish look. Months before, Eve had been shot at. Luckily Mira had been on one of her cruises. Since Eve had promised to stay out of trouble, she'd scrambled to get the bullet hole in the wall covered over before Mira returned. Of course, she'd underestimated her aunt who clearly didn't miss anything.

"No one is going to aim a gun at me. It's been taken care of. We gave it to Jack."

Mira chortled. "I'd hate to be an alarmist, but where there's one gun, there's bound to be another."

Out of the corner of her eye, Eve caught sight of someone hovering by the door. "Elsie?"

"Sorry to interrupt. We... that is, Eleanor and I, we were wondering if we could get a lift back to town." Elsie raised her hand. "There's no hurry. By the way, your guests are leaving."

Eve left Jill to decide if she could spare the time to drive out to town and made a beeline for the dining room. Peering out the window, she saw Miranda Leeds and her husband waving to someone on the veranda. Eve had to crane her neck to see who it might be. As she did, she saw the author striding down the steps and heading toward one of the cars. Moments later, Liz Logan joined him and they drove off.

That left...

Julia Maeve and Martha Payne.

"What's going on?" Jill asked as she came to stand beside her.

"Whatever Julia Maeve and Liz Logan were discussing didn't dissuade Liz from leaving. The newspaper editor is still here, as well as Martha."

"This is our window of opportunity. Where's Jack?"

Eve shrugged. "I've no idea. I'm about to develop abandonment issues."

"I hope we didn't chase him away with all our caterwauling."

Eve frowned. "Speak for yourself. I do not wail. In fact, I'm surprised at how contained we were when we confronted Julia Maeve."

"Yes, I think Mischief and Mr. Magoo made more noise than we did."

Eve strode back to the kitchen saying, "I need to feed Mira

and her editor and then we'll roll up our sleeves and... and wring some information out of Julia Maeve."

———————

"Where is everyone?" Eve asked. She stood on the front veranda looking about.

Elsie appeared behind her. "Everyone left a short while ago. "The woman you attacked this morning lingered for a while, but then she took off."

Jill appeared with Mischief and Mr. Magoo trailing behind her. "Sorry, I took them for a walk. Where is everyone?"

"That's what I just asked."

Jill shook her head. "Window of opportunity. I warned you. We should have acted right then and there."

Now what?

"I'm driving Elsie and Eleanor back to town. Do you want to come?" Jill asked.

She'd left Mira and her editor in the kitchen talking about her current book. They'd looked too engrossed so she didn't want to bother them. "I'll grab my jacket."

As she strode back inside the house, she called out to her aunt, "Jill and I are driving into town. Is there anything you want me to get for you?" She gave Mira a few seconds to consider her offer.

"Yes, please," Mira called out. "The article in the magazine I showed you is actually part one. I'm hoping we can get a copy of the next issue. Could you please drop by the bookstore? There are still some boxes in storage there."

"Well, that's a relief. For a moment there I thought you might have wanted me to pick up a cake."

"Do you have any cake in the house?"

Eve nipped her bottom lip. "I'll get some cake. Oh, and if Jack happens to swing by, please tell him I'm very cross with him."

"That's exactly what my mad innkeeper would say, Eve. Would you like to rephrase the message?"

"Maybe I should tell him myself when I see him. Perhaps you can try to get information out of him. We still don't know what poison the killer used on the cigars." She could only think of one reason why Jack would withhold such a pertinent detail. He'd found a lead and he didn't want her to sniff it out.

Chapter Thirteen

"THIS PART of the island seems to have been hit hard." Jill pointed at another tree that had been brought down by the storm and whispered, "I had my doubts about William's house suffering rain damage."

"Ditto." Yet Eve still refused to let William off the hook.

"This isn't the way into town," Elsie piped in. "Are you driving us out to the cliff so you can put a bullet in us and push us over the cliff? I told you we would co-operate. I gave you my word. What more do you want? A blood oath?"

Elsie continued to play her role to the hilt, and she seemed to be enjoying herself.

Eve exchanged a knowing look with Jill and growled under her breath. "How can we be sure you won't talk, Elsie?"

"Would I risk losing the opportunity of holding my Sisters in Crime Book Club at your inn? I wouldn't dream of it. It's the perfect setting."

"She's cunning," Jill murmured. Leaning in, she asked, "Where are we going?"

"I want to swing by William Hunter's house to see how many of them decided to stay." Jack hadn't mentioned anything about asking them to stay on in the island. What if they'd all decided to leave?

"You won't be able to see the house from the road," Elsie said. "It's set well back and close to the cliff."

When Eve's cell phone rang she asked Jill to answer it.

"It's Abby," Jill said. "She wants to know if we all made it through the night."

"Tell her to meet us at *Tinkerbelle's*. She can help us hunt down the boxes for Mira." As the previous owner of the bookstore, Abby would have a better idea of where to look.

Not wanting to miss the entrance to the Hunter estate, Eve slowed down. When they reached it, she stopped. The gates were open. They'd barged in on her so she didn't see any reason why she couldn't do the same. Checking for traffic, she turned in.

"Pay attention," Elsie whispered to Eleanor Parkinson who sat quietly next to her in the back seat. "I believe we're about to witness Eve Lloyd in action."

Eve rolled her eyes. "Pity you won't be able to report any of it."

When they reached the end of the drive she had two choices. Either drive around and out again, or park the car. She decided to stop long enough to count the vehicles parked.

"They're all here." She could have sworn Julia Maeve had taken off.

"Aren't you worried they'll see you?" Elsie asked.

"I want them to know I have my eye on them," Eve couldn't resist saying.

When Eve drove off, Elsie could not have sounded more disappointed. "Well, that was a bit of an anti-climax. I expected more from you, Eve Lloyd. Perhaps your reputation has been blown out of proportion."

As they neared the town, Eve had to ask for directions to Elsie's house but the woman clammed up saying, "I'm not aiding and abetting you."

Jill sighed and whispered, "I'll guide you." When they arrived, Jill turned and eyeballed the two women. "Elsie McAllister, don't make me get out of the car and drag you out."

"Fine. We'll go peacefully." She waved a rolled piece of paper. "I helped myself to one of your posters. I'll see you at the afternoon tea party."

They drove the short distance to *Tinkerbelle's* Bookstore in silence. Eve suspected their late night was finally catching up with them. "Remind me to swing by the bakery and pick up a cake for Mira, please."

Even before they entered the bookstore, Samantha and Aubrey Leeds waved to them from behind the counter.

"I've been telling Aubrey all about yesterday. I hope that's okay," Samantha said.

Eve nodded. "You know what, you girls can be our eyes and ears in town. Miranda and her husband, Marcus, appear to be book lovers. With any luck, they might come into the bookstore to browse. Do your best to eavesdrop. They might let something slip."

Abby Larkin strode in and stopped in the middle of the store. "I miss this place. Do you think Mira would sell it back to me?"

Eve only then realized she hadn't asked Abby about her efforts to land herself a husband in the city. "Are you seriously thinking of moving back to the island?" When Abby shrugged, Eve added, "You can't have your house back. I'm sorry, Abby. It's mine. Too much has happened for me to lose it now."

Abby laughed. "Don't worry. I wouldn't dream of it. It always felt too big for me. Helena invited me to move in with her or stay at her place on weekends." Jill clapped her hands. "Okay. Let's go hunting for those boxes. I think I know which ones Mira wants." Looking over her shoulder, Jill asked, "What happened to your face, Jill?"

"I was assaulted. Actually, I was also bitten."

"You girls lead such exciting lives. I should seriously consider moving back to the island."

Following a few steps behind, Eve said, "I feel awkward asking for an update on your foray into the dating game."

Abby chortled. "At the rate I'm going, I might end up a spinster. You seem to have struck it lucky with Jack. Jill's done well too. And it's strange, because you both met them during murder investigations so it was a case of the wrong place and wrong time. Maybe I'm trying too hard. Neither one of you went out of your way to entice someone new into your lives." Abby clicked her fingers. "I think I've just had an epiphany. I just need to stop trying and let it happen." She opened a door and stepped back to let them in. "Would you believe it, this is all stuff left over from the time I took over the store from my mom."

Thankfully, all the boxes were labeled, but there were so many, Eve stopped counting at ten.

"We should start looking here," Abby said pointing to a gap. The first couple of boxes were filled with house and garden magazines, but they struck it lucky with the next one. "I think this is the box Mira wants." Abby pulled the flaps open and smiled. "Yes."

"Let's play it safe and go through it," Eve suggested. They found more than they'd hoped for. "Mira wanted part two but she didn't realize there was a lead up to part one." The article covered the week preceding the birthday bash. "The Hunter entourage spent an entire week hitting all the hot spots in Manhattan." She skimmed through the article looking for names. "They were all there."

"Why do you sound surprised, Eve?" Jill asked, "I'm sure we'll all still know each other in twenty years' time."

"Speak for yourself, I might have developed a case of some dreadful disease that will probably be a blessing in disguise making me forget all this."

Jill smiled. "I think it would be fun to reach old age and still be hanging around with the same people. Except for Samantha, I never see anyone from school anymore."

"Why exactly does Mira want this article?" Abby asked.

"We're trying to nail down a theory, but it's still early days. Everyone in the Hunter group knows each other from way back and we're thinking something might have happened and, all these years, they've been keeping a secret. We also suspect there's some sort of dissension from within the group. Someone might be trying to break the bond."

Jill made a crunching sound. "Or tear apart the cone of silence. I hope they realize the truth will set them free."

Abby smiled. "Is this where you suspect everyone?"

"We're all guilty of something," Eve said, "It's just a matter of scratching the surface and finding something significant."

Jill nudged her. "What are you guilty of, Eve? Come on, out with it."

"Me?"

"Yes, you."

Eve sighed. "I guess you'll find out sooner or later. I've gone on sugar-free diets and, I'm ashamed to admit... I've cheated."

Abby gave her a pensive look. "So, if you are capable of a tiny infraction, does that mean you have it in you to take it up to the next level and commit a heinous crime?"

Eve gave it some thought. "I'm sure there's a study somewhere proving some criminals have humble beginnings."

Jill nodded. "Watch out for anyone torturing defenseless creatures and sneaking candy bars after lights out."

Wondering what else would drive someone to commit murder, Eve decided to add vanity to the mix of greed, revenge and jealousy.

"These are all well to-do people. Why would anyone want to jeopardize a comfortable lifestyle?" Abby asked as she flicked through a magazine.

Eve and Jill looked at each other and smiled. "In the course of our accidental investigations, we've come across warped motives. Greed tops the list. Revenge is another reason."

Abby huffed out a breath. "You'd have to be harboring some serious resentment to kill someone."

Eve returned the magazine she'd been perusing to the box. "That's what distinguishes the average person from killers. Having said that, who knows what drives someone to commit murder. I guess that's what temporary insanity pleas are for. We might as well take the whole box with us back to the inn."

"It's lovely to hear you calling it an inn," Abby said. "I was afraid someone might buy the house, tear it down and build a modern monstrosity."

Jill poked around some of the other boxes. "We should take some more back with us, Eve. It'll be lovely to have some old magazines to flick through. I usually have to wait until I go to the dentist to do that."

They each took one box and strode out to the store.

Jill stopped abruptly. "Was that Elizabeth Rogue?"

"Where?"

"Leaving the store."

They both set the boxes down and rushed to the window.

"It is. She's getting into that sporty car. No, wait. She's going to the bakery." Turning back to the counter, Eve asked, "Did she buy anything?"

Samantha nodded. "She came in to get a handful of books. It's strange. She just picked them off the shelf without even looking at the titles."

"That's odd behavior, even from a non-book lover," Jill said. "Do we have any reason to suspect her?"

"If we do, I wouldn't know where to start digging for information about her. We struck it lucky with the others because they're all prominent social butterflies." They'd only skimmed the surface, Eve thought. Who knew what else they'd find if they put their minds to it...

"And yet, Elizabeth Rogue is here with the group. She sat at the table with them. She might be William's personal assistant, but she also engages with his friends. If we hunt around some more, we're bound to come up with something," Jill suggested and looked around the store. "Do you stock magazines?"

Samantha shook her head. "Not the gossipy ones."

"What are you hoping to find?" Eve asked.

"You never know. A photographer might have caught her looking askance at William. You can tell a lot by the way a person looks at someone."

"Are your sales receipts itemized?" Eve asked.

Samantha nodded and handed her the sales receipt, but it revealed nothing. The titles appeared to be random selections.

"Maybe the guests are growing bored and need some entertainment. William has only just moved in. He might not have any books in the house." Jill tapped a finger on the counter, "Or, she purchased the books as a ruse. This could have been her excuse for coming into town and she's now on her way to meet an accomplice. Let's put these boxes in the car and go to the bakery. She might still be there."

Doing something as innocuous as buying a cake, Eve thought. Turning to Samantha, she asked, "How did she pay for her books?"

"By card. She had quite a few of them." Samantha shrugged. "I'm always intrigued by anyone who carries more than one card."

Jill grinned. "More work for Jack if he's going to do a background check on her, as I'm sure he will because you're going to insist there's something suspicious about her."

Eve didn't want to shoot down the idea because Jill might be onto something. "It's always the quiet ones you have to be wary of. I'm sure Jack is already on it. Remember, he still needs to find out who purchased the cigars."

When they strode into the bakery, they were all surprised to find Elizabeth still there. She'd settled at one of the tables to read a newspaper.

While Eve placed an order for a carrot cake, Jill sidled up to Elizabeth and casually looked over her shoulder.

"She's pretending to read The Bugle," Jill reported.

"How do you know she's pretending?" Eve asked.

"She was inspecting her nails. She could be waiting for someone or plotting her next move. Or, our drive into the Hunter house set alarm bells off."

Eve dug inside her handbag and drew out her cell. Nothing from Jack. How could he leave her out of the loop? She sent him a text reminding him to look into the personal assistant's background. To her surprise, he responded straightaway.

"He's already looking into her."

"Who?"

"Jack." Eve frowned as another message came through.

"That made you frown. What does it say?" Jill asked.

"He wants to know what type of cake I'm getting." Eve looked up and out the window. Spotting Josh across the street, she shook her head. Had he been trailing her or Elizabeth? "Josh is reporting our every move."

Jill gaped at him. "The double-crosser."

Elizabeth hadn't moved from her table.

Eve paid for the cake. "Let's head back and start digging through those magazines."

"I'll follow in my car," Abby said. "I can't remember the last time I had so much fun. I'd kick myself if I missed out on something important."

"I think we've become complaisant," Jill murmured as they drove off. "I don't recall ever being that excited about investigating a murder."

"We're doing no such thing."

"Okay, if you say so, but I reserve the right to have the last laugh when we catch the killer."

"From the inn? Once we get there, we're not budging." Eve had enough to keep her busy. With the guests all gone and with no staff available until the official opening, she needed to tidy up.

Jill tilted her head in thought, "Jack must have a good reason for posting Josh in town. Do you think he was actually told to keep an eye on Elizabeth?"

Before Eve could answer, her cell rang. "This must be serious. Jack's calling instead of texting. Can you answer it, Jill?"

"Hello. You've reached Eve Lloyd's cell. Please state your business." Jill hummed a tune. "Jack? Jack who? Oh, Detective Jack Bradford. You wish to speak with Eve? Well, I'm afraid she's busy at the moment and can't take your call." Jill gasped. "That's quite a temper you have, detective." Jill pressed the cell against her chest. "He says you should get your butt over to the inn and stay there until he says it's okay for you to leave."

"Why?"

"Eve wishes to know if she's under house arrest." Jill turned to Eve, her lips forming a perfect O. "He says the revolver you gave him this morning doesn't belong to Martha Payne."

"Who's is it?"

"It's registered to Julia Maeve. She had her own means of self-defense."

Eve tightened her hold on the steering wheel. "So... Where's Martha Payne's revolver?"

"Someone else must have taken it. It's quite possible they'll use it to frame Martha."

"Did Jack say that?" Eve asked.

Jill grinned. "No, that's my very own conjecture, but a sound one, if I do say so myself."

"Tell Jack..." Eve bit the edge of her lip, "Tell him, I told him so. He should have frisked them all while he had the chance."

Chapter Fourteen

"SORRY IT TOOK SO long to get back," Eve said as she set the box of magazines down in the living room. "While you get started with these, I'll put together some lunch."

Mira rubbed her hands and smiled. "Fabulous. Jordan and I need something to take our minds off my current book. Taking a break makes me more eager to get back to work."

Eve smiled in agreement although she never quite understood what her aunt meant when she made those sort of remarks. As a chef, she couldn't imagine walking away from something she was in the middle of cooking...

Jill followed her to the kitchen. "You're not going to mention the revolver?"

"There's no need to worry Mira. Besides, we're not the targets."

"Do you think the killer will strike again?"

"It's not so much what I think, it's how the guests acted."

Suspiciously, Eve thought. "We now know two of them were armed. Why?" Eve inspected her pantry and wondered how much effort she wanted to put into cooking. From experience, she knew Mira would be happy to settle for a sandwich and, if Eve pushed her, some potato salad. "How about some smoked salmon sandwiches?" Eve swung away from the pantry and headed for the refrigerator. "Or a quiche." She had all the necessary ingredients and making pastry always helped her to relax. "Yes, a quiche. Spinach. Mushroom and smoked salmon." She smacked her lips. "The local butcher smokes his own salmon. I've never tasted anything better." She brought out the ingredients for the pastry and noticed Jill paying close attention as she tipped some flour into a bowl.

"You're not measuring."

Eve smiled. "I'm using my years of experience scale. It's infallible. Why are you frowning?"

Jill dug around the cupboards and brought out a scale. "How much flour do you think you put in there."

"Two hundred grams."

Eve stood back as Jill weighed the flour.

"Well, *whaddaya* know. It's exactly two hundred grams."

"I told you. While the recipe requires that amount, I might not end up using it all because flour tends to change from packet to packet. So I have to play it by ear, or rather, by touch. Once I start working the mixture, I'll know if it needs more, or less flour."

"Okay, I'm done questioning your judgment. Can I help with anything?"

"You could wash some lettuce for the salad."

Moments later, Jill asked, "Why are you putting the pastry in the refrigerator? It's going into the oven. What's the point of keeping it cool."

"The pastry has to rest." She tipped some nuts into a bowl to munch on. "Let's go see if Mira's found something useful." Hearing the scrunch of tires on the driveway, she steered them toward the front door, "That must be Abby. I was starting to worry about her."

Not Abby...

Eve didn't bother hiding her surprise. "Hello, Elizabeth."

William's personal assistant lifted her chin slightly. "I need to impose on you one more time. One of the guests lost her earrings. Would you mind if I take a look around? She says she removed them in her room."

Eve drew in a calming breath.

Jill pressed against her and whispered, "Frisk her first."

Elizabeth's eyebrows rose slightly.

"Yeah, you heard me right. If you want to come in," Jill said, "I'll have to frisk you first."

When Elizabeth took a step back, Eve braced herself. Would she make a run for it?

Her shoulders rose and fell. "Fine. I need to find those earrings."

"Spread your arms out," Jill said. "Hand over your handbag first. Eve will look through it."

As Jill frisked Elizabeth Rogue, Eve glimpsed inside her handbag. It felt too light to carry a revolver so she handed it back and offered a light apology. "Sorry, you understand we've been through enough already."

Elizabeth surprised her by offering a small smile. "I'll be as quick as I can be."

"We should go with her," Jill suggested.

Eve tugged her along. "She's not carrying a weapon and she's as happy to be here as I am to see her here. Not..." Just as she was about to close the front door, Abby pulled up.

"Sorry, I swung by the bookstore and grabbed some more boxes."

"Better out than in?" Jill asked, "As in, better here than clogging up the storeroom in the bookstore you hope to regain possession of?"

Abby grinned. "Would I be so devious?"

"No, that's what makes it perfect." Jill smiled. "Now that I think about it, you'd make an ideal killer, flying under the radar because you're just not the type to commit murder. We'll have to keep an eye on you."

They all headed for the living room where they found Mira and Jordan taking notes.

"We've identified everyone on the photos," Mira said. "That leaves one person with a question mark."

"Who?"

"This one." Mira pointed to a woman. She appeared in one group photo standing on the edge and almost looking out of place. In another photo, she hovered in the background. "These photos were taken in Manhattan. William has his arm around her on one. The caption identifies her as his girlfriend."

Eve nibbled on a nut. "You sound dubious."

"Well, you'd think she would feature in the Rhode Island pictures, but she doesn't. He must have dumped her."

"Is she someone prominent?" Jill asked.

Mira shook her head. "I've been going through these magazines and seen the others in the society pages, but not her."

Eve drew in a steadying breath. "What if... What if something happened to her?" She looked at Jill. "What was the name of that movie you mentioned earlier?"

"I know what you did last summer." Jill shivered. "I think you're onto something."

Jordan sat back and gazed out the window.

They all looked at him.

Jill asked, "Is that his thinking face?"

Smiling, he straightened. "I seem to recall one of my authors discussing a case. He's a crime writer. I'll ask him." Jordan got his cell phone out and sent a text message. "I have a vague recollection of a society murder case that remained unsolved."

Eve sat forward. The room burst with excitement. Everyone talked at once but with no names to connect to the unsolved crime, they eventually calmed down.

After a moment of quiet, Eve asked, "Drinks, anyone?"

Mira checked her watch. "It's not quite midday."

"And your point is?" Eve laughed.

"Well, it's not the thing to drink before midday."

"That depends on where you are," Jordan said. "If you're in Denmark, it's quite appropriate to drink *Gammel Dansk*. In fact, the bottle reads, enjoyable in the morning, after a day's work, when hunting or fishing, or as an aperitif. In Germany, it's traditional to have a beer and sausage before midday on Sundays and holidays. In Britain, alcohol etiquette is overturned on Christmas morning when it's considered appropriate to have that first glass of champagne while presents are being opened."

Eve looked at Mira. "We could start our own tradition making an exception because we're trying to find a killer. Bloody Marys would be too obvious."

"In that case," Mira smiled, "I vote for Martinis. It's a classic and the drink of choice for sleuthing."

"I don't think agent 007 is a sleuth," Eve remarked as she dug out some glasses. When she set a tray on the coffee table, Abby hooted with excitement.

"The box I brought has some of the issues preceding the ones we've been looking at and there are more photos of William and the mystery woman."

"Mystery woman or not important enough to be named?" Jill asked. "Everyone else is identified by name. Why isn't she?"

Because she didn't really belong to William's social set, Eve thought. She turned to Jordan, and asked, "Have you heard from your author friend?"

"Not yet. He's in the middle of a book so he might not surface for hours."

"Keep looking, people. The dots are there. We only have to join them. I'm going to finish making the quiche."

She set the oven to preheat and then rolled out the pastry and placed it in a tart pan. As she didn't want the flavors to over-power the salmon, she only sliced half an onion and a handful of mushrooms, which she cooked in a skillet.

With the eggs whisked, she added the heavy cream and continued whisking until it was light and fluffy. Abby joined her just as she was adding the salt and pepper.

"There's something different about you. I noticed it last night. When you get in your kitchen, you transform yourself."

"In a good or a bad way?" Eve asked.

"Oh, definitely in a good way."

Eve smiled. "It's my comfort zone. I know exactly what will happen here. Maybe that makes me a control freak."

"Absolutely not. We all need some sort stability in our lives, something we can easily relate to without having to think too much."

"Let me guess, the bookstore is your comfort zone."

Abby sighed. "I'm lost without it. When you first came to the island you said you could afford to have some thinking time. I'm over it now and quite bored. I guess I'd fail at being a lady of leisure."

Eve shrugged. "It's the way we're conditioned. I've been working from a young age and can't imagine ever giving it up. I know Mira will continue writing until she draws her last breath."

Eve tossed the smoked salmon into the egg mixture, added some shredded cheese and after making sure it was all combined, she pricked the tart shell and poured the mixture into in. She put it in the oven and checked the time. "All done." She made quick work of clearing up the kitchen and putting things away. Everything in its place and a place for everything... Eve frowned.

"What?"

"I just had a thought." Digging out her cell from her handbag, she called the bookstore. When Samantha answered, she asked, "Which shelf did Elizabeth Rogue get the books from?" Nodding, she thanked her and disconnected the call.

"What was that about?" Abby asked.

"Comfort zone." She gestured for Abby to follow her back to the living room. "Mira, when you want to buy a new book, where do you head for in the store?"

"It depends on what I feel like reading," Mira said.

"So you know where the historical romances are shelved."

Mira nodded.

"But you sometimes enjoy reading other fiction. And they're usually shelved in their own sections."

"What are you getting at Eve?" Mira asked.

"When I want something in my favorite grocery store I know exactly where to find it. But if I'm in an unfamiliar store, I have to search. What if I don't care what I want? I only want to buy something. Where would I go?"

"The nearest shelf to you," Jill said.

"Exactly. So, we know Elizabeth grabbed a selection of books without even looking at the titles. She didn't care what she was getting. Why then did she go to the back shelves closest to the door leading to the storeroom?"

They all stared at her.

"How do you know she did that?" Mira asked.

"I just called Samantha."

"But what made you think to ask?"

"Elizabeth's behavior struck me as odd," Eve said. "Anyhow, if she just wanted to grab some books, pay for them and get out of the store, she would have gone straight for the closest shelves."

Jill huffed out a breath. "I feel I dropped the ball. Why didn't I think of that?"

"You would have, eventually," Eve assured her.

"Do you think she saw you go into the store and followed you in?" Abby asked.

Eve nodded. "I'm sure of it. And then she tried to eavesdrop on our conversation."

"What do you think prompted her curiosity?" Mira asked.

Eve exchanged a sheepish look with Jill. "Who knows?"

Jill laughed. "Eve drove right into the Hunter estate waving a red flag. I guess it worked. She must think we're onto something."

"It doesn't mean she's the killer," Mira offered. "She might be doing legwork for the others."

"That would be taking her personal assistant duties to the extreme. We're talking about colluding with a killer." Eve picked up one of the magazines. Could there be a connection between Elizabeth Rogue and whatever happened all those years ago? She gave a slow shake of her head. What if Elizabeth had only been curious to hear their conversation? With everything that had been going on, she might have wanted to be kept in the loop.

"Please don't do that," Jill said. "If you have a theory, we want to hear it."

"How old do you think she is?" Eve asked.

"I'm guessing late twenties and doing very well for her age. I've met her type." Jill rolled her eyes. "Super-efficient."

Abby leaned forward. "Eve, you didn't actually tell us what you were thinking."

"Liz Logan suggested everyone in the group had reason to want Stew dead. We know the entire box of cigars was contaminated." And Jack would get an earful from her for withholding information. She still didn't know which poison was used. "What if someone wants everyone in the group dead? Someone driven by revenge."

"Revenge for what?" Mira asked, her tone intrigued.

For whatever happened all those years ago, Eve thought.

"You're doing it again. Think out loud," Jill insisted.

Eve jumped to her feet and strode around the living room. Swinging back, she picked up one of the magazines.

"What are you looking at?" Jill demanded. "I'm about to get snarky with you."

"The woman."

Jill sprung to her feet. "What about her?"

"I don't know," Eve's voice hitched. She wanted to say there could be a connection between the woman and Elizabeth Rogue, but it sounded too far-fetched. "I have to check on my quiche." Distracted by the thoughts whirling around her mind, Eve strode into the kitchen, her gaze lowered. When she looked up, she tried to yelp but her throat constricted.

It's just a revolver, Eve. You've had one pointed at you before. Don't freeze now.

She couldn't believe she'd actually opened the door to the killer.

"Don't make a sound," Elizabeth Rogue whispered and signaled with her revolver toward the back door.

A good sign, Eve thought. She only wanted her and not the others. Once they were outside, Eve could try to...

What?

Be a hero?

She'd find some way to disarm her and if she made enough noise, it might alert the others. They'd be quick to take action.

The plan unfolded in her mind, leaving no room for doubt. She could do it.

Eve raised her hands signaling her surrender and willingness to follow instructions, but she couldn't quite bring herself to move. Her legs simply refused to obey.

"Eve, I think I have a theory you might like," Mira said from the living room.

Eve saw Elizabeth step back. The gun remained pointed at Eve who prayed Mira wouldn't come into the kitchen.

"Did you hear me?" Mira called out.

"Yes, I'll... I'll be there in a minute." Biting the edge of her lip, Eve nudged her head toward the door.

Yes, by all means, let's do this. Right now before anyone got hurt.

"I think you'll like this." Mira's voice drew closer.

No, Eve mentally shouted for Mira to stay in the living room.

"What if Elizabeth Rogue can be connected to the mystery woman? The idea is so wild, it's right up your alley and I think you'll love it. I'm thinking William was somehow responsible for the woman's death. I know we should wait to hear from Jordan's author friend about that unsolved murder case, but I've caught your bug and I'm happy to let my imagination run wild. Here's something else you'll like. Wouldn't it be just perfect if Elizabeth turned out to be William's daughter seeking her revenge? I should take note and include this in one of my books. Anyhow, seeking her revenge for... let me think, her mother being scorned. What do you think of that idea?"

"It sounds good," Eve called out. "I'll be there in a minute."

Mira came around the corner and smiled.

Eve tried to warn Mira with her eyes but she'd already caught sight of Elizabeth. More precisely, Elizabeth's revolver.

"What on earth is going on here?" Mira asked, her tone more intrigued than surprised or even scared.

"Everyone. Come into the kitchen and see this," Mira said.

Oh, Mira... No.

Jill, Abby and Jordan hurried in.

"This is interesting," Jordan said.

To everyone's credit, they all remained calm.

Jill murmured, "We outnumber her, Eve. We've got this."

Elizabeth's eyes widened. She made a threatening gesture with her revolver. "Everyone listen up. Make a false move and I will fire."

Mira tilted her head. "How did she get in?"

Jill shrugged. "Eve and I let her in earlier. You must have been busy talking with Jordan. Then we got busy and forgot about her. She tricked us saying she needed to look for a pair of earrings. A likely story. I actually frisked her. Where did that revolver come from?"

Eve wished they'd stop moving. She could see Elizabeth's revolver wavering between one person and another.

"Earrings?" Mira asked. "So does she think we stole them?" Mira's chin lifted in defiance. "We would never sink so low."

Eve rolled her eyes. Either Mira was playing a deliberate game of innocent or she had no way of gauging the dangerous situation they'd all landed themselves in.

"I want everyone to just be quiet." Elizabeth pointed her revolver at each person.

"How did she get that revolver?" Jill asked. "Honestly, I did a thorough job frisking her."

"Maybe it was in the house all along," Mira suggested.

Elizabeth pointed the revolver straight at Eve. "Control them or I will."

"Hey guys. Let's do as she says."

"You know as well as I do she can only shoot one of us," Jill said.

"Are you volunteering?" Abby asked.

"Actually," Jill said, "I think Jordan is the largest target. He's taking the bigger risk. I hope he's light on his feet. If we all disperse at once, she won't know where to point and shoot."

Mira cleared her throat. "Should you be saying all that out loud? Now she knows our plan."

"What do you want?" Eve asked, her tone puzzled. Elizabeth Rogue? A killer? "You're obviously looking for something. You didn't come here to kill us. Let us help you."

Elizabeth appeared to be thinking about it.

"Whatever you're planning, keep in mind this is an island. There's only one way out and the bridge is it. Detective Bradford has a patrol car stationed at the other end."

"Why did you kill Stew Peters?" Mira asked.

"Mira!" Eve warned.

"Well, we're just standing here. She might as well tell us. Especially if she's going to shoot us. If I'm going to die any time soon, I wish to know."

Elizabeth gave a brisk shake of her head. "I didn't kill him."

Jill whispered. "That's what they all say."

"Hang on. Let's hear her out," Mira said.

"She's threatening to kill us. Of course, she killed Stew Peters."

"I want the information you have," Elizabeth said. "Everything you've found. I want it. Now."

"Why?" Mira asked.

"Because we're obviously onto something," Jill said. "She probably thinks she can get rid of the evidence and then do away with us. She might even set the inn on fire to get rid of any DNA proof."

"Jill. Don't give her ideas," Abby said.

"You found proof. I want it." Elizabeth pointed the revolver at Jordan. "And you."

"Me?"

"Yes. Your author friend has information too."

"She was eavesdropping," Jill growled.

"And once you have the information, what do you plan on doing with it?" Mira asked. "You'll have to forgive my curiosity, I'm an author."

Elizabeth paled. Her eyes shimmered. "I need that information," she screeched. "Now."

"Wait a minute. There's something wrong here." Eve's cell phone beeped a message.

Everyone shifted slightly.

Eve looked at Elizabeth steadily. "That's Detective Jack Bradford. He's headed this way. If you leave now, you'll have a head start."

"I'm not going anywhere without that information. I can't believe it. All these years spent trawling through every archive..."

"She's crumbling," Jill murmured. "Here's our chance."

"What information is that, dear?" Mira asked. "We'd love to help, but you need to tell us more."

Elizabeth sagged slightly.

Eve frowned and whispered, "I don't think she's the killer."

"What makes you say that?" Abby asked.

"She's looking for a lead. She's on a trail for information. Why does she need it?"

"Because she's somehow linked to that woman," Jill suggested.

They all looked at Elizabeth.

Her eyes flinched. Eve couldn't help thinking it would have been a perfect opportunity to throw something at her but she had nothing handy. For once, keeping a tidy kitchen worked against her.

Elizabeth looked about her as if suddenly snapping out of a reverie. "She was my mother and they killed her."

"Oh," they all said in unison.

"So you then sought your revenge by killing Stew Peters," Mira mused.

"No!" Elizabeth's eyes widened. "I didn't kill him."

"Oh, really?" again, they spoke in unison.

They all exchanged looks and finally Mira asked, "Then who did?"

Elizabeth's lips pressed together, her eyes narrowed and her voice sharpened. "One of them. All of them. I don't know."

Mira gave her a warm, understanding smile. "You have our sympathies, my dear. We're in the same boat. We suspect them, but we can't put our finger on which one did it and why. Now, why don't you put that silly gun down and we can all sit down and talk this through. If we all put our heads together, I'm sure we'll come up with something."

Jill nudged Eve and whispered, "Can you believe Mira has taken the spotlight away from you?"

Eve's cell phone rang. "That's Detective Jack Bradford. He's actually calling so he means business. If I don't answer, he'll worry and head straight here."

Elizabeth scooped in a breath. She took a step forward and gesture to the cell. "Answer it, but remember I'm holding a gun. Tell him you're busy."

Eve nodded and answered the call. "Jack. What's up?"

"Josh followed Elizabeth Rogue to the inn. He says she's still there."

Eve gave Elizabeth a told you so look. "Yes. She's looking for a pair of earrings," she said trying to gain Elizabeth's confidence. "Should I be worried?"

"We don't think so. She's been working for William for five years. I don't think a killer would wait that long to strike. But she could set a precedent. I'll feel better when I know she's left the inn."

"Have you followed the cigar trail?"

"We're close. I've spoken with the water delivery guy and his supervisor. The cigars were couriered to them, which in itself is odd."

Hearing that, Elizabeth frowned. Eve made a mental note to ask her about it.

"What about you? Have you come up with anything?" Jack asked.

"Yes. I think so. Mira had a hand in unearthing some information you'll be interested in. In fact, you need to get onto it straightaway." Elizabeth took a warning step toward her.

"Look into an unsolved murder case. It happened twenty-eight years ago in Rhode Island."

"I think I know the one you mean. Give me a minute."

Eve hummed under her breath and ignored Elizabeth's gun.

"Alicia Bennington," Jack said. "She drowned. The police closed the case saying it was an accidental drowning. Her family insisted there was foul play, saying she never went into the water because she couldn't swim. The police didn't find any evidence to convince them to re-open the case."

"Is there mention of a daughter?" Eve asked.

"She'd recently had a baby. Alison Bennington."

Eve looked at Elizabeth Rogue. A splotch of deep crimson spread across her cheeks.

Had she changed her name in order to infiltrate the group and find out the truth?

"Eve? Is something going on there?"

Eve smiled and, keeping her tone cheerful, said, "There's always something happening here. You know me, Jack. I'm a magnet for trouble with a capital T." She hoped he caught on to the message. So far, she'd been grumbling about always being labeled a suspect. Surely Jack would find it odd that she should suddenly sound cheerful about it.

Elizabeth made a wind it up motion with her gun.

"I have to go, Jack. I'll see you tomorrow." Eve decided Jack couldn't possibly miss that underlying message.

Elizabeth snatched the cell away from her. "Into the living room."

"What a good idea," Mira said. "We should all get comfortable and talk. Get to know each other better..."

They all started moving with Elizabeth bringing up the rear.

Despite what Eve had learned, she didn't care to have a gun pointed at her. The situation could get out of control at any moment. If she didn't do something...

In that split second, Eve swung her arms and yelled, "My quiche is burning."

Chapter Fifteen

IN THE NEXT SECOND, Eve wished she'd had a better idea.

Her elbow connected with Jill's nose.

Fortunately, not all was lost.

Clutching her nose, Jill reacted by falling back and colliding with Elizabeth. Caught by surprise, Elizabeth fell back and her hip connected with Eve's new stove.

Mira, bless her soul, snatched the revolver from Elizabeth's hand. "I'm sorry, dear, but you have no business pointing that thing at us."

Still clutching her nose, Jill nodded and mumbled, "Well done, Mira."

"I wasn't going to shoot you," Elizabeth wailed.

Surprised by the uncharacteristic emotion spilling out of the young woman, Eve helped her up and said, "We know, but we really don't react well to having guns pointed at us. Now sit down and we'll talk."

"Should we tie her up?" Jill asked.

"She won't go anywhere. We have information she wants." Or, at least, Eve thought they did.

"I'm sorry about... about the gun. It just happened. I really did come here looking for Martha's earrings but then I found her revolver."

Elizabeth continued by explaining she'd come down the back stairs and had heard them talking. Eve had then gone into the kitchen and she'd panicked.

Jill leaned forward. "Have you actually been working under cover all this time?"

Elizabeth nodded. "It took me a year to land the job. My persistence paid off. I spent all that time learning all I could about William Hunter and his friends." She shook her head. "I could never find anything to incriminate them."

Eve showed her the magazines and asked, "Do you recognize any of these people?"

Elizabeth gave a stiff nod and then she saw the photo with her mom in it. Her eyes shimmered. "All these years... They've been getting away with it. I had to do something."

"Did that involve killing Stew Peters?" Mira asked again.

"No." Her gaze remained on the photos. "Where did you get these from? I've been trawling the Internet and libraries for any sort of image that could connect my mom to them."

Elizabeth had probably done a thorough job of it, but with so much information out there, it would have taken a small army to go through years of magazines. Even if the search was narrowed down to that timeframe. There was simply too much to trawl through.

Instead of answering her, Eve said, "Detective Bradford mentioned other family members."

Elizabeth nodded. "An aunt and an uncle. They gave up hope a long time ago. That's when I took up the search."

"What do they remember of that time? Was your mom in contact with them?"

"My mom wouldn't talk about my father or the people she socialized with."

Had Elizabeth joined the dots? Could they assume William was her father? Eve looked up at the ceiling and hoped it hadn't been Stew Peters.

"How did she meet them?"

"She'd been working as a waitress. My aunt only knew she'd taken up with the wrong crowd. All those parties and wild weekends, she knew it would all end badly." Her hand shook as she traced the outline of her mom's image.

"Why did she say that?"

"My mom was an outsider. She didn't belong with them. My aunt knew the man she'd become involved with had only been toying with her."

Mira discreetly moved one of the magazines out of Elizabeth's way. Eve guessed it was the one with the photo of William with Elizabeth's mom.

"My aunt finally convinced her to stay away from them. One weekend she said she was going to work at a function to earn extra money. She never came back."

Had Alicia Bennington confronted her baby's father?

Or had she confided in someone?

Eve shot to her feet.

"What?" Jill asked.

"My quiche. I forgot again." She rushed to the kitchen with Jill following on her heels.

"What do you make of all that?" Jill asked.

"Can you picture any of them welcoming an outsider?"

Jill shook her head.

Eve took the quiche out of the oven and set it on a cooling rack. "Jill? When did William marry his first wife?"

Jill's mouth gaped open. "No. Really?"

Eve nodded. "How do you think she would have reacted to the news of another woman snatching William away from her?"

"Not very well. She's well known for having a bad temper."

Eve played around with the idea of Alicia Bennington confronting her baby's father, but it didn't stick. Despite her negative impressions of William, she suspected he would have acknowledged paternity and taken care of Alicia. She then tried to imagine someone else in the group as the father.

The author?

No. He too would have acknowledged the baby.

Stew Peters?

She hoped not.

Deciding it had to be William, she wondered what his then fiancée would have thought if she'd found out.

Valentine.

A killer.

Yes, Eve could see her pushing Alicia Bennington off a jetty or a boat. But what about Stew Peters?

Eve looked at Jill. "Stew Peters must have witnessed her doing the deed."

Jill gave a vigorous nod.

"Bravo."

They both turned.

"For heaven's sake. Really? I'm getting tired of having guns pointed at me," Jill muttered.

Valentine stood by the kitchen back door.

"Hey, where did you get that gun from?" Jill demanded. "That's one gun too many."

"Shut up. I knew you were trouble when I saw you taking photos of us."

"For heaven's sake. What do you think you're going to do?" Eve asked. "There are too many of us here. Are you going to shoot us all? Or is this your way of working up to a plea of temporary insanity?"

Valentine stood firm for a second. Then she bit the edge of her lip.

Eve laughed. "Yeah, I can tell you didn't think this through."

"You killed Alicia Bennington. Admit it," Jill demanded.

"The next person who opens her mouth gets a bullet," Valentine warned. "And—"

She didn't get a chance to finish.

A vase flew across the kitchen and hit her on the nose.

Eve and Jill lunged for her and grabbed hold of the gun. To their surprise, Valentine fought back.

They all rolled around screaming at each other until Jordan put a stop to it all.

"Stop or I'll shoot you in the face."

Valentine immediately covered her face.

Jill groaned. "She barely flinched when the vase hit her nose and now she cowers?"

"She's probably had nose jobs done," Eve said as she straightened. "I'm told they're quite painful. She must have developed a resistance to pain." Turning, she saw Mira and Elizabeth standing by the door. "Who threw the vase?"

Mira smiled. "My editor. Isn't he good? He played high school football."

The next few moments were chaotic as Jack stormed in with his officers who'd all responded to a call from Josh.

"I think your inn has experienced a baptism by fire," Jack said the next day.

"Oh, Jack. Please don't mention fire. That's the one thing we haven't had here."

"That's not entirely true," Jill said. "Surely you remember the mad woman who threatened to get rid of all the evidence by setting fire to the inn?"

Oh, yes. Eve had forgotten about her. "Let me get this straight," Eve said, "William cheated on Valentine and then she found out Alicia Bennington had a baby and killed her."

Jack nodded. "Valentine forced Alicia Bennington into a rowing boat. She rowed them out and then pushed her off."

"She must be mad. What sort of woman makes a child an orphan?" Eve slumped back on the couch. A vain and selfish one, she supposed. "We guessed Stew Peters must have witnessed it all. Were we right?"

Jack nodded. "The others were witnesses too, but they were too far away to do anything to help. Apparently, the author tried but he was too late. Stew Peters convinced them it didn't look good for any of them, so they all decided to stick to one story. Complete silence. None of them had seen her in weeks."

Fear of discovery had kept them together. With each passing year, they knew their continuing silence made it impossible to come forward with information.

"Did none of them think of her daughter?" Eve asked. "Or her relatives."

"They didn't know about her. Valentine was the only one who knew of her existence."

"I can't believe William went ahead and married her," Eve remarked.

Jack smiled.

"What?"

"I really don't want to rain on your parade. You seem intent on pinning something negative on him."

"Go on. Ruin it for me."

"For starters, he didn't know about the baby. As for Alicia's drowning... He really thought it was an accident. Valentine convinced them all Alicia had become hysterical and had tried to kill her. Valentine had only just announced her engagement to William and she said Alicia had tried to warn her off him."

"And they believed her?" Jill asked.

Jack shrugged. "That's their story, and they're sticking to it."

"What's going to happen to William?" Eve asked.

"He withheld vital information so he'll have to answer to

that, but he can afford the best legal counsel so I doubt it'll cost him much."

"How do they feel about Valentine now?" Eve couldn't imagine they'd be happy about her lying to them all these years.

"They've cast her adrift. She too can afford legal representation." Jack finished his coffee and smiled at Eve. "Are you going to join the other dots?"

Eve rolled her eyes.

"Come on, you can do it."

The cigars, Eve thought. "I'm really having trouble with that one. The entire box poisoned with ricin? Valentine would not have wanted to kill William. She'd already killed Alicia to get her out of the way." Eve looked over at Jill who shrugged.

"I'm all out of ideas too."

Eve tapped her chin. "I remember we wondered about the cigars William smoked."

Jack nodded.

"Am I getting warm?"

"Maybe."

"You said he always carried two cigars with him." If she wanted an answer, she knew she had to ask the right questions. "There's something about his cigars that set them apart from all other cigars." The man drank exclusive water. He led an exclusive lifestyle. "The lure of the forbidden," Eve mused. "Cuban cigars?"

"Rolled by hand and smuggled in specially for him. He never smokes any other cigar and only one person knew that."

Valentine.

"She overheard Elizabeth organizing the purchase and

delivery of the water so she had the box delivered to the company with an enticing bonus to deliver it."

"Where did she get the ricin from?" Jill asked.

"Mira's editor said with the right instructions anyone could make it. I somehow doubt that," Eve said.

"Valentine paid an old boyfriend who works as a chemist to produce it for her. With enough money you can buy just about anything."

"But why did she decide to kill him now?" Eve asked.

"You were right about Stew Peters. He kept them in line and he enlisted Julia Maeve to help him. Every now and then, he'd play at pulling the rug from right under them, threatening to reveal everything he knew to the police. Valentine decided to take matters into her own hands."

"And now it's out in the open." Being in the newspaper business would help William cover it all up. Today's news would become a distant memory in no time.

Jack looked down at the floor and then at Eve. "Are you pressing charges against Elizabeth Rogue?"

No, she couldn't. "I think she's gone through enough and she still has some way to go. Has she found out who her father is?"

"They have to run a paternity test, but William insists he is her father."

"Argh! I hate the man. He's deliberately thwarting my attempts to dislike him."

Epilogue

"YOU'RE IN LUCK. The sun's shining and there isn't a single cloud in the sky." Jill pirouetted around the living room. "We have two more days to go and then the doors will officially open to your first paying guests."

Meanwhile, they had the entire population of Rock-Maine Island to entertain. Every surface in the kitchen was filled to capacity with trays of food. Eve had been baking since the crack of dawn and loving every minute of it.

Eve put down her copy of The Bugle. She'd been scouring the local newspaper looking for Eleanor Parkinson's first article about the inn to no avail. Either the town chronicler had kept her word and had decided to write a sanitized version of events, or she was biding her time, waiting to catch Eve by surprise. Either way, if anything ever happened to Eleanor Parkinson, Eve knew the finger of suspicion would be pointed directly at her. "I have to admit, I was a little apprehensive at first thinking no one would want to come." Eve pushed back the curtain. "Who are all these people? Anyone would think I'd hired a crowd."

"They're all locals."

"Really? I only recognize a handful. I'm almost afraid there won't be enough food. You can't possibly know all these people," Eve said.

"Did you just use your wary tone?" Jill laughed.

Three deaths at her inn. Strictly speaking, they had taken place at the house she had transformed into an inn.

Once she opened the doors to the paying guests, she could start with a clean slate. Eve nibbled the edge of her lip. "That woman looks suspicious."

"That's Claire Owens. She's a teacher. I can vouch for her. I've known her all my life."

People had been arriving in droves since mid-morning. Thinking there might be some interest in walking through the inn, Jill had suggested having some entertainment for the children, hence the pony rides, clowns and face painting.

"I have to admit, I'm feeling a little uncomfortable having so many people I don't recognize walking through."

"You're afraid there's a killer out there staking out the place." Jill pointed toward the end of the front yard. "I have people posted strategically around the inn. See, there's Josh. He and his police buddies are keeping an eye on everyone."

"Who's that woman by the pony rides?"

"That's Marcia-Lee. She's a regular visitor to the island. Oh, look. She brought her granddaughter, Shayna, with her. She's adorable."

"Yes, she is gorgeous. Do you think I'll ever become a granny?"

"Nothing is going to go wrong, Eve. Put it out of your mind." Jill nibbled the tip of her thumb. "Granted, the granddaughter could be a decoy used to distract us while Marcia-Lee snuffs someone out." Jill laughed. "Actually, I can vouch for her too."

"Are you sure?"

"Absolutely."

Eve pointed at Elsie McAllister. "Elsie's headed straight for Marcia-Lee. I still don't trust Elsie to keep quiet. And look, she's handing out pamphlets. I bet they're for her Sisters in Crime Book club. I have a good mind to ban her from the inn. We should intercept her. You have to admit, Elsie has a perfect cover and she could be looking to enlist someone's help to carry out the perfect murder."

"You need a distraction, Eve. Look over there. There's Roger McLain. Didn't you say you were going to give him an earful of your angst for suggesting you would single-handedly bring shame upon the town?"

"I certainly did. Come on, let's grab a tray of cupcakes. One of them might find their way to his face."

"Oh, I love that. Food fight."

Made in the USA
Monee, IL
14 April 2020